Love Released - Book Seven
Of Women Of Courage
Love Released Serial
By
Geri Foster

Love Released
By Geri Foster

First Edition

Copyright 2015 by Geri Foster

ISBN-13: 978-1517387402

ISBN-10: 151738740X

Cover Graphics
Kim Killion
Lilburn Smith

All rights reserved. Without limiting the rights under copyright reserved above, no part of this publication may be reproduced, stored in or introduced into a retrieval system or transmitted in any form or by any means (electronic, mechanical, photocopying, recording, or otherwise) without the prior written permission of both the copyright owner and the above publisher of this book.

Author contact information: geri.foster@att.net

This is a work of fiction. Names, characters, places, and incidents are either the product of the author's imagination or are used fictitiously. Any resemblance to actual persons living or dead, businesses, events, or locales is purely coincidental.

Thank You

Dear Reader,

Thank you for reading *Book Six of Women of Courage, Love Released*. I know venues are filled with many authors and books and the choices are limitless. I'm flattered that you choose my book. There are additional books in this series and if you enjoyed Cora and Virgil's journey, I hope you'll read the others.

If you'd like to learn when I publish new books, please sign up for my **Newsletter** www.eepurl.com/Rr31H. Again, I appreciate your interest and I hope you'll check out my other books.

Sincerely,
Geri Foster

       Visit me at:
       www.facebook.com/gerifoster1
       www.gerifoster.com/authorgerifoster
       www.gerifoster.com
       Join us for discussion of Women of Courage @
https://www.facebook.com/groups/689411244511805/

GERI FOSTER

ACKNOWLEDGEMENTS

    This book dedicated to my husband, Laurence Foster. After all these years you're still my one and only love. Thank you for your support, and for believing in me when I had doubts. You've shown me that dreams really do come true and love isn't just in romance novels.
    Always,
    Geri Foster

LOVE RELEASED

CHAPTER ONE

Cora heard the words spill out of her mouth but still couldn't believe she was pregnant. How could that be possible after the abortions she'd been forced to endure while in prison? A quick glance at Virgil told her he was as surprised and bewildered by the news as she was.

Hand to her mouth, Cora fought back tears of utter joy because she never thought she'd say those words in her lifetime.

Pregnant.

Was that even possible? Could there be a mistake? It would break her heart to get her hopes up only to have them dashed by a miscarriage in the near future.

Virgil came to his feet, scraping the legs of his chair on the tile floor. "What did you say?" His handsome face brightened and his mouth curled into a cautious, yet delighted smile that disappeared as quickly as it began.

Looking up at him, Cora batted back tears that threatened to shatter her soul into a million pieces. "Dr. Richie said I'm going to have a baby."

His brows pulled together tightly, wrinkling his forehead. "But you said you couldn't..."

She held up her hands, praying her heart would settle down to a normal pace. "I know what I said. And I believed I was telling the truth." Placing her palms on her desk, she came to her feet. "Oh, Virgil, I never imagined."

Before she could restrain the tears further, Virgil came around her desk to pull her into a powerful embrace that nearly sucked her breath away.

They'd just been given the most wonderful gift and Cora found it difficult to accept such a miracle so quickly. Her mind struggled to process this unexpected news in the world.

Suddenly she felt light and giddy, as if the happiness inside her couldn't be contained. Burying her face in the warmth and security of his neck, Cora silently considered her good fortune.

His hand gently cupped the back of her head as he leaned close to her ear and whispered, "You make me the happiest man alive."

She stepped back, still clutching his arms. "I'm so much in love with you, Virgil. I can hardly contain the way I feel."

Glancing down at her stomach, he grinned. "Hard to believe there's a new life growing inside there, isn't it?"

She followed his gaze. Her loose white lab coat covered her clothes and any sign there was a baby present. "Yes." Their gazes clashed. "We have so much to talk about."

"Jack," Virgil said. "How do you think he'll take the news?"

With everything happening so fast, she hadn't the time to think about her nephew and his reaction, but it was a valid concern. "We'll have to make sure it's a very special occasion and that he's involved from the beginning."

"You're right." Virgil cocked his head and averted his gaze, appearing deep in thought. "Where in the world will we put a baby?"

"In our room, of course," she replied. Even now, the thought of having a wall between her and their child made her tense and nervous.

"But later, when it's bigger. We don't have another bedroom."

She squeezed his forearms then reached up and turned his face toward her. "I don't want to move."

He leaned forward then kissed her on the nose. "Neither do I."

"Well, what will we do?"

"I'll think of something," Virgil said confidently. "Don't you worry about anything except having a healthy baby."

She smiled and placed her palm on her tummy. "A baby," she whispered.

"Hard to imagine, isn't it?"

A nervous chuckle escaped from between her lips. "It's practically impossible."

The phone on her desk rang, intruding on their small celebration. As she answered, she noticed her husband looked as if he'd grown two inches in the last five minutes. The grin on his face could light up Main Street.

"Hello?"

"This is Ethan. Is Virgil there? It's an emergency."

Cora didn't waste any time handing the phone to him. A moment after the receiver touched his ear, the smile slipped from his face. He dropped the phone and turned toward the door.

"It's a cave-in at one of the mines."

As he disappeared from sight, Cora called out, "Keep me posted."

Doctor Adams was on emergency duty today so she wouldn't have to go to the scene, but she sent up a silent prayer that there would be no injuries. She'd never experienced a mining incident but plenty of the residents of Gibbs City had, and it often devastated the families involved.

Alone, Cora slumped down in her chair then leaned back, releasing a deep sigh. With fingers pressed to her temples, she tried to comprehend coming to terms with Dr. Richie's announcement. What if she wasn't able to carry the baby to term?

No! The thought sent her heart pounding erratically, and her throat constricted so tight she thought she might choke. No matter what happened, she had to have this baby. The thought of having a miscarriage frightened her to the point she feared her legs wouldn't hold her.

Even in the short time since finding out about being pregnant, she'd fallen in love with this child. Gathering her composure, she allowed her mind to go there.

The thought of holding a newborn in her arms filled her heart so full of joy she thought it might burst. The very idea had her head spinning, and clutching the edge of her desk to try to settle her nerves.

Dr. Richie had been very clear. So far the pregnancy was normal, and all indications were she'd have a healthy normal baby. And that's what she intended to concentrate on.

Squeezing her eyes tightly, she stood, blinked back the gathering tears then left her office. She took the elevator down to the cafeteria to buy a bag of chips, because she suddenly craved something salty. Not that she was hungry, but because she'd hardly eaten anything for the last couple of weeks. Silently she ticked off the months.

If Dr. Richie's calculations were correct, she must have conceived on her wedding night. Thinking back to that weekend, Cora could certainly understand if that were the case. After all, they'd waited to have sex until they exchanged vows and were on their honeymoon.

After the ceremony, they'd left Jack with Maggie, and spent the weekend at a hotel in Joplin. They'd had no time for a real vacation, but they certainly didn't complain. Being with Virgil had exceeded her expectations.

She'd never experienced anyone so loving, caring or giving in her whole life. It wasn't difficult to believe that during that magical moment she'd gotten pregnant.

Yes, dreams really did come true.

Dr. Stan Lowery came to her table wearing his usual white lab coat with a red bowtie. He nodded politely then pulled out a chair. "Nice to see you eating again," he sounded as authoritarian as every other doctor would be talking to a patient. "Nutrition is very important to everyone."

Dying to shout her news to the world, Cora smiled. "I've been diagnosed."

Taking a sip from his bottle of soda, he bit off a chunk of a Tootsie Roll. His face darkened and he slumped into the chair beside her. "Oh? Anything serious?" he mumbled around the candy.

"I'm pregnant."

He stopped chewing, his mouth split into a chocolate-covered-teeth smile. "That's great news."

"It is, because I honestly didn't think it was possible."

"Well, I'm very happy for you and Virgil. I bet he's over the moon."

"That's putting it lightly." Reaching in the bag for more chips, her chest burst with sheer joy. "We're both very happy."

"I bet."

"Oh, by the way, Stan, have you heard anything about the mining accident?"

Shaking his head, he glanced out the large window where the ambulance usually parked. "Not a thing yet. I'm sticking around for a while should the doctors on call need help."

"I'll give Maggie a quick call so she can keep Jack."

"You don't have to stay." He reached over and squeezed her hand. "There's a baby to consider."

"I'm fine and I want to help. That's why I became a doctor."

"We can't do much until word arrives from the scene and the attending doctor notifies us." Stan took a drink of his RC Cola. "They can be really bad. I personally would hate working underground."

"I think those who take that kind of work do so because there's no other choice."

"You're right. Every man feels obligated to care for his family. Unfortunately, sometimes that means risking your life."

Cora left and finished her regular rounds. Several patients had been discharged that morning, and aides were busy getting the rooms ready for the next occupants. Hopefully, today's accident at the mine wouldn't take up all the beds.

Waiting for news, Cora turned and headed for her office. On the way she ran into Nurse Mae Price, the fire chief's wife.

"Have you heard anything yet?" Cora asked. Mae was one of the best nurses on the staff at Gibbs City General and Cora was glad they were friends.

Wearing a tense expression on her normally pretty face, Mae shook her head. "Not a word. We're all hanging around should they need extra help." She sidestepped a cart full of laundry being pushed down the hall. "I hope we're fully prepared. God only knows what's happened in that hellhole."

"The mines are horrible."

"They're graves that haven't been filled in yet." Mae looked away. "My father was killed in one of those pits when I was just a young girl. I don't remember a thing about him. I was only two or three."

Touched by her grief, Cora put her arms around Mae and hugged her. "I'm so sorry to hear that. It must've been sad growing up without a father."

Although Cora had sympathy for the nurse, her own father had been less than a person. He wasn't ever a real parent to her. Instead she'd been ignored most of her life.

"It was," Mae said, "But my mother and my grandparents made a home for us. When I left for nursing school my mother re-married. I never really cared for the guy, but she was happy." A buzzer went off and Mae turned toward the room with the red light above the door. "Gotta run."

Cora watched her walk away, realizing for an instant she'd forgotten she was pregnant.

LOVE RELEASED

CHAPTER TWO

Virgil arrived at the Lucky Lady mine and squealed to a halt next to the fire truck. Grabbing a black helmet, he exchanged it for his tan Stetson and stepped out of the squad car. At a run, he made it to the entrance where Frank and Ethan waited, looking down the huge hole in the ground.

The first words from Virgil's mouth were, "What are we looking at here?"

Frank held his hard hat by the chin strap as he waited for the men to get out the hoisting cage so it could be lowered back down to haul up more men.

"We're waiting to see if there are any injuries. It appears a chamber of the mine collapsed. Right now, no one knows how many men, or if any are trapped below." Frank's breath fogged in front of his face. "We won't have a count until the last of the men comes to the surface. Those workers closest to the cave-in will be up last."

Ethan looked around at the growing crowd, moving his feet to keep them warm in the snow. "People are awfully worried. Every time the cage is hoisted up, there's a cry of relief for some, and fear grows worse for others."

"We don't know how many are trapped yet?" Virgil asked.

"We haven't heard a word." Frank pointed to the foreman, who stood talking to the owner of the Lucky Lady, Arthur Bridges. "He's not exactly sure where the cave-in happened because he wasn't below at the time. He'd just returned with a box of dynamite he planned to send below."

Virgil looked at the bleak surroundings and cringed. The snow around the area was trampled and black, the landscape barren and empty, except for a big derrick that housed the hoisterman, a damned hole in the ground, and rigging lines that moved men, supplies and ore in and out of the mine.

Since some mines were so deep in the ground, the big cage lowered the men ten at a time. There were always two men on the platform to make sure the men didn't get out of the cage until it'd come to a complete stop and they could safely exit.

The underground boss, Winston 'Cap' Heatherly came toward them, gasping for air. "We're the last. The rest are on the other side of the cave-in."

Arthur came closer, his face etched with concern and sorrow as he faced Winston his crew chief. "Cap, who's down there?" Arthur glanced at the derrick.

Not able to meet his boss's gaze, Cap kept his eyes on the toes of his shoes. "I don't know, sir. I was on the sublevel, but I think its Dabney Colson's crew."

"How many men did he have with him?"

"Usually four to six, but at least one had been sent to work helping the hookers."

Arthur patted Cap on the shoulder and said, "Go get some coffee and stand by. We'll need your help."

All the miners who'd made it out were standing, waiting. Some wore their hard hats with the familiar carbide lights on top. Dust covered them from head to toe, but they all waited like everyone else. Miners created deep bonds and looked out for and protected each other while underground.

Virgil held up his hand to get everyone's attention. "Who knows what happened down there?"

Ron Graves stepped forward. "I was right next to the south corridor when the timbers just crumbled." Ron shook his head and looked down at the frozen ground. "A few seconds later and the shaft filled with rock."

"Who's trapped down there?"

"Four men I know of." Graves confirmed. "They're beneath a good ton of rock."

Frank moved next to Ron, grabbed him by the arm and turned the man to face him. "Did you hear voices? Anyone try digging them out?"

"It was too dusty," Cap spoke for his man. "After the shaft collapsed, you couldn't see anything or breathe."

Frank put on his hat and buttoned his coat. "What about the last ones out?" Several men held up their hands. "Do you think anyone is alive down there?"

No miner wanted to say what he thought. The problem with lead and zinc mines was when they caved, usually that part of the earth dropped down, leaving it hard for anyone to survive. They all knew the risks and so far, in Gibbs City, they'd been luckier than others.

Now, maybe they weren't so fortunate anymore.

A voice in the back said, "It would be a miracle."

They watched dust drift up from the shaft, then Frank signaled to the hoisterman. He climbed in the cage along with Virgil and Ethan. Later, when the miners weren't so shaken, they'd probably join them.

Virgil couldn't imagine how it felt to work beneath the ground and constantly worry about it falling in on you. That took a special breed of man, and he wasn't equipped mentally for that. To experience a massive cave-in when you're in the earth's bowels must be a frightening and unforgettable thing. He'd learned that sometimes fear of it happening again ended miners' careers. All too often it was the wives who begged them not to go back down for fear of becoming widows, and with good reason.

For now, he, Frank, and Ethan would check out the damage and see if there was anyone alive down there, and if they could get to them. Once the miners' nerves settled, they'd be down there right beside them, helping to rescue their comrades.

Virgil's heart raced and he closed his eyes on the descent. There was nothing like being dropped into a hole in the earth to make a man want to give up his breakfast.

Frank put his hand on his shoulder. "It won't be long."

"I'm fine once I hit solid ground," he said, but he had trouble convincing his stomach.

"I hate these mines," Ethan said. "They remind me of being pinned down by enemy fire. You have no place to go."

The cage landed softly on the ground, but the dirt had yet to settle. It swirled in the air like tiny gnats, as grit filled their eyes and noses. They stepped out and went in the direction of the southern corridor.

In order to get to the site they had to take what the miners called a *goat's trail*. A narrow path cut into the rock wall that connected one level to the other. Half-way there Virgil saw cracked stone walls and water seeping through the crevices. A sure sign of a recent cave-in.

At the chamber, they climbed over a mound of rock and rubble that would later be broken down to chat. Inside that ore was where the lead and zinc hid.

Further down the path, they noticed another stack of rubble, but this one spilled out from the passageway that led to another part of the mine.

"I think we're at the site," Frank said, looking around for a shovel. "I see pieces of the framework that collapsed."

Ethan grabbed a pick and Frank a shovel. Virgil tapped on the wall. "Anyone there?"

Not a sound came to them except the echo of Virgil's voice. It took four tries before a faint, distant tapping reached them.

Virgil held out his arm for silence. "Listen, I think someone's alive."

"I heard something, too," Ethan whispered. "It's so weak, it's barely there."

"That's enough," Frank said. "Let's get busy."

Virgil and Frank shoveled as much debris out of the way as they could. Ethan chipped away at the rocks that were now so tightly compacted together they couldn't move them.

Every so often one of them tapped on the wall to reassure whoever was left that they were coming for them. That was the only time they took a break. Virgil looked up at the hard earth above him and wondered if it would hold. God didn't mean for a man be down there. No one should.

Shoving aside the rocks, Ethan looked up. "Here comes Cap and his crew with their tools of the trade. "

Frank said, "Damn time. The extra men are badly needed to move the rubble aside so we can keep digging."

Several mine hoppers showed up on the scene and they were soon loaded with rock and moved quickly out of the way. Sweat poured off Virgil's face while he continued to work as hard and fast as he could. If those miners ran out of air before they got to them, he'd never forgive himself.

Besides, their families deserved the best every man down there had. It was their duty to do everything possible to save them.

Virgil stopped long enough to call out, "This is the Sheriff. Who's in there?"

"We're back here, Virgil."

He turned to the side, recognizing the voice. "That you, Rannie Murray?"

"It is."

"We're working our way toward you."

"There ain't a lot of air in here and you're a long way from where we're trapped."

"How many are there," Ethan asked. "Anyone hurt?"

The silence made Virgil's concern grow and suddenly he didn't want to know the answer. Didn't want to know how many had given their lives for a damn mineral. "We'll get to you, don't worry."

"I'm sorry to say only two of us are alive. Two are dead, and Roger Freeman has a busted leg."

Virgil shared a discouraged look with Frank as the inevitable hit him in the chest. "You sure they're dead?"

"Yeah, one's at the bottom of a rock pile and Terry Watters got his skull crushed by falling rocks."

"We're coming, Rannie. Just hang on."

A machine man showed up with a rock drill and before long the mine hummed with activity. Men went about shoring up the walls as they dug their way toward the waiting miners. Virgil couldn't help but wonder if they'd make it in time. If the men were trapped in an air-tight chamber, they could be out of air in a matter of minutes, depending on the size of the compartment.

Stripped down to their bare chests, every man dug with any piece of equipment he could find. Drag men and hopper pullers filled hopper after hopper with rock and rubble away from the cave-in. They moved them out quickly and efficiently. Mining was hard work and Virgil admired these skilled workers as they desperately tried to save their friends and fellow miners.

Working frantically, they finally reach the trapped men. Leaning against the back wall, they were covered in grime and sweat plastered their hair, but they were alive. They helped Rannie and Roger out first. Ethan and several miners went up with them to make sure they got the help needed. With his leg broken, Roger was in a lot of pain and had to be hauled up on a stretcher. Then the rest of the men surfaced.

In the last cage, Virgil and Frank loaded the bodies of the two young miners and took the slow trip to the top. Terry Watters and Sam Ruth were good friends. Virgil had known them since they were born. Both men were single and living at home with their parents. Virgil had heard the two men were looking to rent out the apartment the old bank secretary, Harriett Turner, lived in before she went to prison for embezzling.

The families of the two deceased waited patiently, not breaking down until they were able to see for themselves that their loved ones had died. Terry's father held his wife as they both cried. Off to the side, Sam's father fought back tears as his wife became hysterical and dropped to the ground. As Ollie knelt beside her, he shoved away any help from those close by.

LOVE RELEASED

An ambulance took Roger to the hospital to get his leg fixed, and Rannie sat on the running board of Virgil's squad car. The undertaker, Herman Buckley, waited in the distance. When people decided to go home, he'd come over and collect the bodies.

Arthur expressed his condolences to every miner and their families. "I promise an investigation into how we can prevent it from ever happening again."

Clutching his wife against his side, Sam Ruth's father spit at Arthur's shoes. He pointed toward the Lucky Lady. "That was a death trap when I worked here years ago. You should've closed that damned thing."

Arthur pulled his coat closer. "I stay in constant contact with the Department of Safety Engineers and I welcome them to inspect my mines any time they please."

"That don't mean nothing 'cept you pay off the inspectors."

Ruth walked off, anger trailing in his path. Arthur rubbed his face and heaved a hard sigh as he approached Virgil. "I feel horrible about this. I've been meaning to sell these damn mines. They keep me up at night."

"I don't know if selling the Lucky Lady would've prevented this. But I do wish we didn't have these holes in the ground."

"I agree," Arthur said. "Lucky Lady, my ass," He looked at the derrick. "Cursed Lady would better describe the place."

Virgil noticed a young man, with a clerical collar talking to Lyle Watters and his wife. Could that be the new minister? He spoke softly and escorted them to their vehicle. Then he came closer to the mine.

He held out his hand. "I'm Daniel Washburn, the new minister. I'm sorry we're meeting under such conditions."

"Virgil Carter, County Sheriff." He pointed to the other men. "This is Frank Price the Fire Chief, Ethan Mercer is my deputy and this is Arthur Bridges. He owns the mine."

The tall, dark haired man with sharp brown eyes and hands the size of baseball gloves tipped his hat and smiled kindly.

"I'm pleased to meet you gentlemen. I'm going to stay here and help Mr. Buckley load the bodies."

"That's kind of you," Arthur said. "If you need help, let me know."

"I will and I hope I'll see you all in church day after tomorrow."

As he walked away, Virgil looked at Frank. "He seems nice enough."

"He's a hell of a lot better than Fuller."

Virgil shook his head. Reverend Fuller had been a mean-spirited man who'd judged Cora harshly and been abusive to his wife. Virgil wasn't surprised when she died that he lost touch with reality and tried to kill himself in their kitchen. "According to Judge Garner, Charles was sent to St. Louis and admitted to an institution. Barely knows his own name."

Arthur paced anxiously as he shoved his graying hair back repeatedly. "God knows we all go through enough in this life. Sometimes, I'd like to forget who I am."

Virgil patted the older man on the back. "This was an accident. They happen all the time in mining communities. There's no reason to make it harder than it already is."

Arthur looked at him with keen blue eyes. "I know, but I always feel responsible. I bought those mines so people in Gibbs City would have work. Now, with two dead young men on my conscience, I regret ever signing the contracts."

Virgil looked up. Several large lights lit the surrounding area. "It's dark. We all have families to go home to."

On the way to his car he thought of Cora's good news today. They were going to have a baby. God, who would've imagined?

LOVE RELEASED

CHAPTER THREE

Cora had just finished putting Jack to bed, and was cleaning the kitchen when Virgil came in the front door. Exhaustion rolled off his slumped shoulders and slowed his footsteps. She ran to him and took his arm for fear he'd drop to his knees. What a morning he must've had. He looked like he'd been working for days.

Cora decided to wait until Virgil was ready to discuss what happened at the mine. She'd heard about the leg injury and the two deaths, but she didn't want to bring it up until Virgil had a chance to catch his breath.

"I have a hot bath ready for you."

She led him into the bathroom, removed his grimy clothes and helped him step into the tub. He was filthy from the top of his head all the way down between his toes.

As he leaned his back against the porcelain tub, she took a washcloth and bathed him. He sighed several times before she convinced him to get out of the dirty water so she could rinse him off with a couple of pans of clean water.

A towel wrapped around his waist, he went into the bedroom and slipped on a pair of khaki's and a clean tee shirt. His shoes were too dirty, so he just slipped on a pair of socks and followed her into the kitchen where she had kept his supper warm.

Slumping down in the chair, he used his hand to prop up his head. "I'm exhausted."

She set his plate down. "You need to eat something then go to bed." She poured him a cup of coffee then went to turn away.

He looped his arm around her waist and kissed her stomach. "Did you tell Jack yet?"

Her cheeks heated. "No, I wanted us to do that together." She turned away and poured a glass of milk. Taking a sip she joined him at the table. "I haven't told a soul except Stan while I was at the cafeteria today."

He looked completely worn out. "I figured the whole town would know by now."

After a moment she shrugged, unsure what to say, and ashamed for being such a coward. "I couldn't even bring myself to tell Maggie."

Putting his fork down, he looked at her, his face a mask of surprise. "Why?"

Picking up the tea towel, Cora twisted the corner. "I don't know." While she didn't want to spoil the perfect news, she also didn't want him living in a false hope. "You know I had several abortions. I may not be able to carry this baby to full term."

He took her hand and brought it to his warm lips. "Sweetheart, there are always risks when a woman is carrying a baby. But you can't go through the next six and a half months worrying that something could go wrong."

"I'm not."

He tilted her chin where she looked him in the eyes and Cora wanted to shrink away. "Yes, you are. Have a little faith. You didn't even think you could get pregnant to start with."

Turning away, she covered her face with her hands. "I know. It's just that I'm so scared."

Pushing back the chair, he stood, and gathered her in his embrace. "We have a right to be a little scared, but what if it all works out fine?"

"Then I'd be very happy."

"So would I." He kissed the top of her head as she wrapped her arms around his waist. "That would be wonderful."

"Let's live with that, instead of thinking of all that can go wrong."

She leaned her cheek on his chest and listened to the strong, steady rhythm of his heartbeat, and wondered how she'd gotten so lucky.

"I promise I'll be better." She pointed to his untouched plate. "Now sit down and eat."

"Yes, ma'am."

"How did things go at the mine? I stayed later than usual should they need extra help, but only one man was injured."

"Yes, but two were killed."

Cora gazed down at her hands, sadness filled her heart. "Earl came over and told me that there had been two deaths."

"How'd he find out so fast?"

She lifted her shoulders in a shrug. "He does have a phone."

"Yeah," Virgil agreed. "And he is friends with Arthur."

"What does Arthur have to do with the mining accident?"

"He owns the mine."

Cora remembered that while she worked at the dry cleaners she'd heard that he had quite a business empire, but she didn't know he was involved in the mining industry.

"I bet he feels horrible."

"He does."

"I'm sorry that I never met those young men. Now I won't see them until their funerals."

"They were too young to die, all right. And Roger Freeman broke his leg and he's too damn old to be working in a place like that." Virgil took a sip of coffee. "I guess a man does what he has to do for his family."

"That's too bad. Earl said he has three children."

Virgil nodded then went back to eating. Soon he finished and she took his plate away only to notice his hands. Turning his palms up, she saw the red blisters.

Frustration filled her chest. Why couldn't she keep her husband healthy? "My goodness, you're barely healed from the fire at Leonard's barbershop, and now, you're hands are torn up again."

"That's from the shovel. We had to dig those guys out." He flexed his hands. "Just hope I don't have to do much tomorrow. I doubt I'll be able to straighten my fingers."

Frowning, she headed for the back porch. "When you get up tomorrow, let's soak your hands in Epsom Salt and see if that helps. In the meantime, let me get some salve for those blisters."

"I had planned to surprise Jack by taking him out to cut down a Christmas tree tomorrow."

She came back to the kitchen table with the tin of medication. "Really, so soon?"

"Well, they're usually put up right after Thanksgiving."

"That's true. It won't be long until businesses start decorating their windows."

Flinching as she smeared on the salve, he said, "But I think I'll wait until next Saturday. There's no way I can handle an ax."

"And I don't want you to."

Earl came into the kitchen and looked at Virgil's blistered hands. "What happened to you?"

Virgil didn't bother to look up. "Shovel."

"I heard Sam Ruth and Terry Watters died."

"They didn't stand much of a chance," Virgil said. "According to Rannie, they were standing right next to the wall when the cave-in happened."

"That's the damned problem with those mines. They're death traps."

"Some people need to feed their families."

"Shoot, I'd rather be mucking cow patties in a barn than down in the ground."

Cora carefully wrapped Virgil's hands. As he started protesting, she stopped and glared at him. "This is just for tonight. I don't want that salve all over the sheets." She finished the task. "Besides, you'll thank me in the morning."

Virgil grumbled, but didn't say too much since she'd left his thumbs uncovered so he could lift his cup.

"You hungry?" Cora asked Earl, putting her medical supplies back in the bag Dr. Westley had given her when she first came to Gibbs City. "There's a plate in the oven for you."

Earl took his plate out and poured himself coffee and refilled Virgil's cup while he was up. "I heard it was a rip roaring time at the mines. Old man Ruth got pretty nasty."

"He'd just lost his son. I'd be the same way if anything happened to Jack."

Earl looked at Virgil and Cora then said, "Jack ain't going in no mines. Not as long as I'm breathing."

Moving closer to her neighbor, Cora put her hand on his shoulder and squeezed. "We don't intend to let that happen. I'm hoping he goes to college."

"That'd be the smart thing," Earl grumbled.

"I like the way you come in here and tell us how to raise our son," Virgil said, sarcastically. "It's like we don't have a brain in our heads."

"Earl means well," Cora said. "He loves Jack."

"We all do, but Cora and I will decide what's best when it comes to Jack's future."

"Okay," Earl barked. Then he stuck his chin in the air. "What's best?"

Virgil looked at her for help, but Cora grinned and walked away. She wasn't going to get between them. There were no two men who liked to argue more than Virgil and Earl.

She reached for the cherry pie that had been kept warm with Earl and Virgil's dinner in the oven, when a knock sounded at the front door. Virgil shoved back, stood and made his way through the living room.

Earl had cleared his plate and stood at the sink getting ready to take dessert dishes from the cupboards. He stopped and turned. Arthur stepped inside, holding his hat in his hand. He looked miserable.

Cora's heart went out to him. "Arthur, come in out of the cold." She covered the distance between them. "Have you had dinner?"

He shook his head as Virgil, with his bandaged hands, tried to help their guest remove his coat. Cora hung up the garment and hat as Virgil guided Arthur to the kitchen table and encouraged him to sit.

"How you doing, Art?" Earl asked. "You look froze to death."

"I can't feel anything."

Cora quickly put a plate of sliced roast beef, potatoes and carrots in front of the man who used to be her boss when she worked at the dry cleaners.

Arthur didn't touch the food. Instead he stared at the wall, his face somber, eyes half open.

"You need to eat something," Cora said. "That will make you feel better."

Arthur heaved a great moan. "I just wish this hadn't happened."

Virgil leaned closer. "What's done is done. We all have to go on."

"But I have the death of two men on my conscience, as well as one badly hurt."

Earl took a sip of coffee and reached for a piece of pie. "You can't go thinking like that, Art. All miners know the risks."

"A month ago Cap told me the beams needed replaced. I sent Dabney to the hardware store that morning. Those timbers should've been fixed immediately."

Virgil looked at Cora. "Are you sure? That might've caused the cave-in."

Arthur gave Virgil a sharp look. "Why would you say that?"

"Often, when those men start reinforcing the framework, it gives out." Virgil put his hand on the table and moved his cup closer. "It's happened before."

"Are you saying it was carelessness on the men's part? They didn't put the new braces in place before tearing out the rotten beams?"

Virgil shook his head. "It's just a thought."

Cora sat beside Virgil, hoping Arthur would eat something. He'd be sick if he didn't get some nutrients in him. Grief did terrible things to a body. She'd experienced that first hand.

"I think you need to try to eat something," she said.

Earl moved his plate closer. "Yeah, Missy's right. You get some food inside you and you're bound to feel better."

"I can't eat knowing those men will never have another meal."

Cora stood and rubbed her hand across Arthur's shoulder. "This is a tragedy, but there isn't anything you can do to erase it. It happened and everyone has to move forward no matter how much it hurts."

Earl cleared his throat and shoved his saucer closer. "If nothing else, have a piece of pie and coffee. You need something."

Arthur accepted Earl's offer and Cora couldn't believe he'd given anyone his slice of pie. She filled the coffee cup and gently took Virgil's injured hand.

As silence filled the small kitchen, Cora thought of the families and how sad they must be. Death was a terrible thing that left behind a void impossible to fill. The loss of two young men with their lives ahead of them would surely affect the entire town.

CHAPTER FOUR

Virgil felt terrible for his friend, but running mines was a risky business and one he wanted nothing to do with. There was money there, all right, but not enough to grab his interest.

Looking at Arthur, he couldn't help but feel his pain and suffering. And the worst wasn't over yet. There'd be wild accusations, people demanding the mines be closed, the union would try to step in and all hell would break loose.

Arthur looked over at Virgil. "Will you go down in the mine tomorrow with the inspectors? I'd like to know they're doing their jobs and that it was purely an accident and there wasn't any neglect on my part."

"I'll be happy to do that. I have to write up a report anyway. When someone dies in the town, no matter the cause, there's always paperwork."

Earl touched his long-time friend's arm. "Don't you worry. This will eventually settle down. It always does."

"I'm closing the mines," Arthur said. "I know it means a lot of men will lose their jobs, but I don't want another person's soul on my hands."

Shaking his head, Virgil disagreed, "Don't be too quick to act. Most of those mines have supported a lot of families and you and the other owners do a tremendous amount of good for the town and the school. Gibbs City needs you. While the work is dangerous, there's new safety measures implemented every day."

"You're right, of course." His hands on each side of his head, Arthur groaned. "I just feel so torn. I can't help but see the pain in those people's eyes."

Earl stood and tapped Arthur on the shoulder. "Let me drive you home. It's been a long day."

Arthur turned and looked at Earl. "How will you get back?"

Earl pointed to Virgil. "He'll follow me."

"No he won't," Cora stated. "Not with those hands. I can drive."

Earl blinked. "You know how to drive a car, Missy?"

She raised a brow and smiled. "Yes I do. I used to own a brand new Oldsmobile."

"Well, I'll be damned. I never knew that."

Virgil chuckled as he helped Cora into her coat. "There's a lot about her you don't know."

They left and Virgil put the dishes in the sink. With his hands all wrapped up like a Christmas present, he couldn't do much, but he didn't want Cora to have to come home and clean. Exhausted, but out of habit, he went into Jack's room to check on him and found Pal sleeping snuggly on the little rug beside his bed.

The minute Virgil entered the room the dog raised his head and wagged his tail. Kneeling down, he scratched Pal behind the ears. "You're a good dog. I don't know where you came from, but Jack sure loves you."

He waited until Cora returned then went into the bedroom. "You need to get some rest," he said. "And when are you going to tell Earl that we're having a baby?"

"I hadn't thought of that. I wonder what he'll think."

"Another someone to spoil, that's exactly what he'll think and do."

She smiled. "I hope so. Since she won't have a grandfather from my family."

"Wait, did you call it a she?"

Cora nodded with a smile. "I sure did."

"You think it's a girl?"

She fell back on the bed laughing. "I have absolutely no idea. I just hope she's healthy and happy."

"Again with the she."

"I refuse to call my unborn child an it."

"Okay, you call her a she, and I'll call him a he." Virgil got undressed. "Whose side do you think Jack will be on?"

Cora slapped him on the back. "Oh, you guys plan on ganging up on me?"

"I'm just saying, maybe this is meant to be a male dominated home."

She rolled over as he sat on the bed. Rubbing her hands up and down his back, she sighed. "I just pray for healthy and normal."

They climbed into bed and Virgil wrapped his arms around his wife and child, secure that his son slept peacefully in the next room. During the hardships of the war, Virgil never imagined he'd be this lucky.

To have a home, a wife, kids and a great job. It had all seemed so far away and yet he was almost living a dream.

The next morning as he removed the bandages, Virgil hissed when busted blisters the size of quarters covered his palms. He figured Frank and Ethan's hands were just as bad. He did manage to make a pot of coffee before Cora left the bed and came in the kitchen to make Jack his special pancakes.

Yes, it was Saturday and it wouldn't be long before the kids would be off for Christmas vacation. Looking at the skillet he smiled up at her. "You know what I want."

She rose to her tiptoes and kissed his mouth, causing his heart to do all kinds of crazy things. "Yes, I do. You want a stack of regular flapjacks. They're coming up after Jack gets his favorite."

Before Virgil could pour the coffee Jack came tearing out of his bedroom, Pal hot on his trail. "It's special pancake day."

Cora leaned down and kissed Jack on the head, his hair sticking straight up. "Good morning."

"I want a double stack today," he said. "I'm starving to death."

"No, you're not. How about one extra?"

"Ah, shucks. I want a stack of special pancakes that reaches the ceiling."

Cora laughed and the sound brought a smile to his face. "I think your eyes are bigger than your stomach, little man."

After serving Jack, she went about whipping up the batter for Virgil. As the grille sizzled he and Jack talked.

"I don't know," Jack said, stuffing half a pancake in his mouth. "What does Aunt Cora think?" he mumbled around a mouth full of food.

"Jack I've told you not to talk with food in your mouth."

The young boy swallowed. "Uncle Virgil asked me a question."

"Then you wait to answer when your mouth is empty."

"Yes, ma'am."

She placed a delicious smelling stack of pancakes in front of him, and Virgil feared he might start drooling before he could take a bite. While he smeared butter and syrup all over the flapjacks, Cora scrambled an egg and toasted a slice of bread in the oven.

As they sat in the warm kitchen enjoying breakfast, Virgil thought he would bust at any minute. No one could cook like Cora. He and Jack were damn lucky.

Picking up his coffee cup, Virgil said, "I asked Jack if we could go next week to get the Christmas tree."

She smiled. "That sounds like fun."

"It does," Jack agreed. "But we ain't got no decorations."

Cora sat up, with the fork on the way to her mouth. "He's right. I don't own a single ornament."

Virgil shrugged. "We'll just buy some in town."

Cora looked sad. "That's not the way it works. Each thing on the Christmas tree has to symbolize something special."

"I didn't know that," Jack said. "I just saw this really pretty picture in a magazine and thought that's the way all trees looked." He thought for a moment. "'Cept, the one in our classroom is really puny and barely has any branches."

"Oh dear. It might be hard to find just the right tree."

Glancing at Cora, Virgil said, "It could be a bad year. Jack and I will have to go out and look around next week. The sad thing is we might not have much to choose from by then."

"I'm sure you could get someone to cut down a tree for you," she said.

Virgil shook his head. "No, this is mine and Jack's first time. We want to do it ourselves." He glanced at Jack. "Right?"

Jack nodded. "Yeah, we've been planning."

Cora took a sip of coffee. "Okay, you men have lots of luck getting the tree and I'll try to get my hands on some decorations."

Jack beamed. "Can we have popcorn wrapped all around the tree?"

"Yes, we can have that."

"What about those fancy, shiny bulbs?"

"Oh, I'm not sure. We'll do our best."

Virgil stood, pulled Cora into his arms for a hot kiss and ruffled Jack's hair. He had to work today. The inspectors would be at the mine by now and he wanted to make sure he could answer any questions the families might have about the incident. God forbid he not do a complete investigation. The townsfolk would have his hide.

Driving through town he arrived at the mine just as Arthur was getting out of his car. He looked worse than he did last night. Dark bags hung beneath his eyes, and if Virgil didn't know better, he'd think Arthur had aged ten years overnight.

Instead of his fine suit and coat, he wore his old hunting clothes of coveralls, thick boots, and a canvas jacket.

He nodded to Virgil and they joined the team of three inspectors. Virgil put his hand out first. "Sheriff Virgil Carter."

There was Jake Rydal, AC Sharpe, and Tub Ebby. They worked for the Department of Safety Engineers and it was their job to make sure mines were safe. Rydal was the lead engineer with a waist as wide as he was tall. Sharpe was darker and looked to be half Indian with high cheekbones. Eddy was the most average guy Virgil had ever seen. He had a medium build, brown hair, brown eyes and bland features. But he did have a nose like a trumpet.

No one spoke until they reached the bottom of the mine. Rydal turned to him. "Were you first on the scene?"

"I was the first man other than the miners. Me, the fire chief and my deputy."

"Where did you find the bodies?" Sharp asked.

"Right this way." Virgil led them to the south corridor and stopped in front of a pile of rubble. "You'll have to climb over this to get in there."

The men moved out while Arthur stayed behind. Virgil imagined he found it difficult to be in the same place the men had died, considering he owned the place they were killed.

Rydal looked around with a flashlight. "These beams are pretty rotten."

Virgil pointed behind him. "There is a pile of planks over there that were to replace them."

"Why weren't they up?" Ebby asked

"I don't know," Virgil replied. That was the question on his mind. It spoke of negligence to him.

"Who's the crew chief of this mine?"

"A guy we call Cap. He's been in these mines for over twenty years."

"We'll need to talk to him."

Virgil nodded. "Other than the timbers, I didn't see any problem down here and I walked the whole tunnel."

"We'll be down here for a while if you want to go up top."

"I've done my job. I wanted to see things for myself so I could inform Mr. Bridges. He and I will be answering to the town's people."

Out of the mine, the three men approached Arthur. He was the man who stood to lose everything. As they drew closer, Virgil saw the concern of Arthur's face.

"It looks like everything is okay. But, Cap should've taken care of those rotten beams," Virgil said.

"I thought he planned to fix them right away." Arthur pointed to the stack of lumber. "Why wasn't it done? The materials are right there."

Virgil shook his head. "That's the big question."

"I was under the impression the timbers were fixed," Arthur said.

"It broke at the load bearing part of the frame, but unless there was something that caused that to happen we're back to the beginning," Virgil said. "Strange how something so harmless could cost two lives."

Virgil took Arthur by the arm and walked away from the mine and said "A lot depends on how this mine was constructed in the first place. We need to go back to your office and see how the mine is mapped out. It could be that something shifted overhead."

When the inspectors were done, they all returned to the surface where Ollie Ruth waited. "You find out why my boy died?"

Virgil walked over and put his hand on Ollie's chest to make sure he didn't go after Arthur or the inspectors. "We don't know anything yet."

"I ain't asking you, Sheriff. I want to hear what these fancy inspectors and the rich owner have to say."

Ebby came closer and stood in front of Ruth. "We've only started. Nothing has been confirmed. When it is, we'll let you know."

Ollie spit in the dirt, and snarled his thick lips. "The hell you will. You're like the rest of those government people. Old man Bridges will slip you a wad of money under the table and you'll be on your way."

"I'd never do that, Mr. Ruth," Arthur said. "I'm heartsick that your son died and I want to get to the bottom of it."

"The hell you do. You want to just keep filling your pockets at the expense of our young men. If the war didn't take them, you do."

Virgil pushed on Ollie. "No one wants that and you know it."

Tears brimmed in the father's eyes. "All I know is my only son is dead." He turned and stomped away.

After he left, Arthur slumped against Virgil's car. "This is horrible."

Rydal came over to Virgil. "We're going to be staying in town for a few days. Once we have all the facts, we'll file a report."

"I'd like you to keep in touch with me. So I can make sure the residents remain calm."

"I don't have a problem with that."

"Also, you'll have to go to Carterville because our only hotel, The Connell, is closed. The owners died and no one can find their remaining kin."

"Not a problem," Rydal chuckled. "I hear the food's crappy around here anyway."

"That would be correct. The food at Betty's Diner is so bad it's barely legal."

Virgil watch the three men drive away and went to talk to Arthur. "There's no need for you to keep grieving like this. You need to go home and get some rest."

"I can't even close my eyes without seeing the bodies of those dead men."

"Why don't you get your daughter Ester, and Alice, and go visit your sister in Joplin for a few days?"

Arthur gave him a sharp glance. "And look like I'm running scared?" Arthur straightened his shoulders and reset his hat. "I'll stay right here and answer any questions the Tribune wants to ask. Never let it be said I didn't do right by those families."

CHAPTER FIVE

Cora had the day off and decided since she was feeling better she'd tackle some much needed housecleaning. Jack and Tommy were in his room as she stripped the sheets off her and Virgil's bed and replaced them with clean ones.

Now that it was winter, washing was a pure nightmare, constantly having to drape clothes all over things in the house and hoping they'd dry. She often took several things to the dry cleaners because she had no time for laundry after work.

The day passed swiftly as she fed the boys soup and sandwiches, before allowing them to go outside and play in the snow for a while. She'd kept a close eye on them from in the house and made sure they stayed out of the street and didn't leave the area.

It was too cold for them to be out long.

Maggie crossed the street bundled in her coat, and once inside she stomped her feet on the back porch floor. "How are you?" she called out. "I came to see if the doctor found anything."

Cora had already put on a fresh pot of coffee and laid out a plate of cookies before Maggie even made it to the door.

"Come in before you freeze." Outside Jack, Tommy and Pal ran laughing and barking through the snow. "Those kids think snow is a toy."

Maggie pulled out a chair and sat down, her fingers wrapped around an empty cup. "They think the same thing about sunshine. Boys just naturally love the outdoors. Briggs is almost fifty and he still loves to go hunting and fishing."

Cora poured the coffee and joined her friend.

Eyeing her with narrowed eyes, Maggie stirred in a little sugar as she followed Cora's every move. Her scrutiny was so intense Cora felt her eyes on her and wondered if Maggie suspected something.

"So, what'd the doctor say?"

Cora didn't want to say anything yet, but with her best friend giving her the third degree, she smiled shyly and picked up a cookie. "I'm going to have a baby."

A smile as bright as the sun lit up Maggie's face. She jumped from her chair, wrapped her arms around Cora's waist and practically bounced her up and down. "I'm so happy for you."

Cora pushed from her grasp and stepped back. "Well, don't shake the baby too much, she's not ready to be born yet."

"I just knew you and Virgil would have a child together. Something told me there would be an addition to your family."

Cora sat down and folded her hands. "I wish I'd known. I couldn't for the life of me figure out what I had. It's a good thing I was sitting down when Dr. Richie told me I was expecting, or I might have collapsed."

"Dr. Richie brought every one of my boys into the world. He's a wonderful man."

"I know." She looked at the person who'd stood by her during some awful times and battled back tears. "After what I've been through, I'd simply put the possibility out of my head."

Maggie leaned closer and took her hand. "What did Virgil say?"

"Oh," Cora chuckled. "His head blew up like a balloon."

Maggie smiled. "That's because he loves you so much."

With her hand on her stomach, Cora looked at Maggie. "I hope I can carry this baby to full term. If anything should happen, I think I'd die."

"Surely God wouldn't give you this kind of hope only to snatch it away."

"I know." She looked out the window at the boys and Pal. "I'm so lucky to have Jack. I feel greedy asking for more. But, Lord, the thought of having a baby nearly takes my breath away."

Laughing, Maggie threw her head back. "It always does. There's something wonderful about bringing another life into the world."

Cora moved closer and whispered, "I'm scared."

"You wouldn't be normal if you weren't. But, have faith that this child was meant to be, and you'll be fine."

"But what if I miscarry and lose the baby?"

Maggie put her palms on the sides of Cora's face and looked her in the eye. "What if you don't?"

Cora couldn't hold back tears any longer as she imagined her holding a tiny baby in her arms. "It would take a miracle."

"They happen every day."

Before the ladies could continue their conversation, the boys and Pal raced into the house, covered in at least a bucket of snow. "It's starting to snow again," Tommy shouted. "We're going to have a blizzard."

Maggie stood. "No we're not. And don't take your coat off. It's time to go home. I have a few things for you to do around the house, young man."

"Aw, Mom, do I have to?"

Slipping her arms through the sleeves of her coat, Maggie smiled at Cora, and she didn't feel so alone. "It's going to be fine." Her friend pointed to Jack with her eyes wide with a question.

Cora shook her head and looked away. They'd tell Jack, but she wanted Virgil there when that happened. Maggie and Tommy left and Cora cleaned up the boys footprints as Jack went into his room and made a half-hearted attempt at picking up his scattered toys.

She had to stay on him for a while, but it wasn't long before she announced his radio program would be on in thirty minutes and if the room wasn't done, there'd be no lying on the couch and listening.

Jack flew into action and Cora wondered why he hadn't done that earlier just to get it over with. Children had a strange way of looking at things.

With most of the house work done, Cora sat next to Jack, with Pal curled up in her lap. They listened to the program for a while, and Cora relaxed when Jack edged up against her and crossed his skinny little legs. How she loved her family.

Her hand on her stomach, she prayed for the safety of the unborn child she carried. Reaching down, she put her arm around Jack and kissed top of his head. She loved him dearly. While she was expecting a baby, nothing would ever replace Jack in her heart.

Virgil stopped by and found them on the couch, the program almost over. Jack jumped up and ran into Virgil's arms. "Did you see the snowman we built?"

"I sure did. That's a fine job."

"We didn't decorate him because we figured he was too small. But we couldn't reach way up to do a good job of putting his head on straight. We needed a ladder."

Sitting on the couch, Virgil put his arm around her shoulders. "Maybe later we can go out and fix the head. Since it's in our yard we don't want anyone thinking we can't do justice to a snowman."

"Yeah, you're right. We have a rep...reput..."

"A reputation to uphold?" Virgil asked.

"Yeah, that's what I meant."

After Jack settled on Virgil's lap, he leaned over and kissed her. "How's your day, sweetheart?"

She looked around. "As you can see, not very productive."

"Oh well, that's okay. We'll survive."

"I was hoping I could talk you into taking us to Betty's Diner tonight for a hamburger."

He reared back and crunched up his face. "I can't believe you like that greasy food that tastes like fried hay."

"I like 'em too, Uncle Virgil. 'Specially the fries with catsup."

"Well, I'm outnumbered, so I guess it's Betty's rotten Diner tonight."

She giggled and pushed herself off the couch. "You want coffee?"

"That sounds good. Got any pie left to go with it?" he asked, following her.

"You're in luck. Earl left one piece of that cherry pie from last night."

Virgil shook his head and tightened his lips. "That mooch just helps himself to whatever he wants."

Jack rose up and came eye to eye with Virgil. "That's because he's family."

Cora felt he'd like to set Jack straight, but a stern look from her had him backing off. Earl was important to Jack and she knew the elderly man would die saving Jack's life. And Cora loved Earl, too. He treated her like a daughter and she was glad to have him in their lives.

Pouring the coffee, Cora took a seat and propped her chin on the palm of her hand. "So, what happened at the mine today?"

"Not much. They're just starting to examine the site. It'll be days before they decide anything." Finishing the pie, he shoved the plate away. "Arthur is really taking it hard. I feel bad for him. That man would never deliberately hurt anyone."

"I know. And he does so much for the town."

"People don't think of that when there are two miners in the morgue. They forget the good things that come out of the mines and concentrate on the harm it does to human lives."

Cora rubbed her forehead. "I'll be glad when it's all over and things get back to normal."

"Yeah, I'm sure Arthur feels the same way."

She smiled brightly. "Besides, Christmas is right around the corner. What a horrible time of the year for something like this to happen. It's just awful."

He reached over and took her hand. "How do you feel?"

"I'm fine."

Virgil glanced at Jack still sitting on the couch. "Don't you think it's time we told Jack?"

She ducked her head and stared at her lap. What if they said something and then the unthinkable happened? How could they explain that? "Maybe we can wait a week or so."

"Why not now?" He kissed her cheek. "My parents are going to want to know."

"I know, I know. It just hasn't sunk in for me yet. Give me a few days to digest the news then if you want, we can put an announcement in the newspaper."

He laughed out loud then pulled her into his arms. "Don't tempt me."

"You two lovebirds," Jack said from the couch. "Always kissing."

Cora looked at her nephew, his nose wrinkled in disgust. "What do you know about lovebirds?" She pointed her finger at Jack. "You just wait. Your time's coming."

"You ain't gonna see me smooching all over some girl." He ran around the house smacking his lips, Pal barking behind him.

Virgil released her. "What about Sally and her five cent kisses?"

"Now she's up to a dime," Jack said matter-of-factly.

Virgil whistled and winked at Cora. "Not worth the money, huh?"

"Nope, I ain't giving a girl no dime for a kiss. A boy would have to be crazy in the head."

Cora sat back on the edge of the couch. "Are other boys buying her kisses at a dime?"

"Nope. Us men have gone on strike."

Virgil knelt down and rubbed Pal's belly. "You hoping she'll lower her price?"

"We don't even care now. Besides, there's a new girl in class and she's prettier than Sally."

Virgil grabbed Jack, put him on the floor and started tickling him. Jack laughed and Pal barked. "You going to be smooching on her?"

"Un-ha." Jack said around a giggle. "She don't like boys."

Cora stood and went to the kitchen. "Smart girl."

Virgil stopped, the room turned quiet. "Now just a minute. You saying a girl who likes boys is dumb?"

Putting her hand on her hip, Cora shook her finger at both of them. "No, what I'm saying is a seven-year-old girl shouldn't be thinking about boys at all. And I bet if Sally's mother knew she was selling kisses, she'd put a stop to it."

"Phooey. Almost every girl is thinking about a boy," Jack said. "Even the new girl. She's just pretending."

Cora lifted her chin. "How do you know, young man? You able to read minds, now?"

Earl came in, putting a halt to their discussion about girls and boys as Jack went to his room. "What did they find out today, Virgil?"

"Not much. They'll be here a few days, checking on stuff."

"I just came from Arthur's and he's too upset to do anything. Ollie Ruth came while I was there but I ran him off. The damn hothead."

Virgil poured two cups of coffee. "He's always been that way."

Earl sat in front of one cup and took a sip. "Just like his daddy. But, unlike him, Ollie is all smoke and no fire. Never saw the man land a punch."

Virgil's brow wrinkled. "Neither have I. He's been in plenty of arguments."

"Now, his daddy was a real bruiser. On Saturday nights he'd get so liquored up, he'd try to take on half the town. Don't know how many times he landed in jail."

"When I was away in the war, I wasn't surprised when my buddy Carl received a letter from home saying some guy from Baxter Springs had stabbed Ollie's dad with a knife and killed him."

Earl's grey hair stood on end when he'd pulled off his hat. "I remember that being an awful mess."

"Arthur still talking about closing down the mines?" Virgil asked.

Earl nodded. "Right now his head is a jumbled mess. He's so wrapped up in grief."

Cora came and joined them at the table. "That's normal. Even if he shouldn't, I'm sure he feels guilty."

"I hope they don't find any problems in the mine. That will only feed the fire," Earl said. Cora noticed he sipped his coffee slowly. No doubt his mind was on his friend's problem.

"I heard from the hospital that Roger Freeman's leg is going to mend well and besides being on crutches for a few weeks, he'll recover completely."

Earl braced his hand on his thigh and looked out the kitchen window. "Not going to be fun in this damn weather."

Cora agreed. "You're right, but he should be fine."

"He's a heck of lot better than Ruth and Watters."

Virgil rose to his feet and went to the stove. Picking up the coffee pot, he shook it. "There's one cup left. Who wants it?"

Cora and Earl shook their heads, so Virgil emptied the pot in his cup before returning to his chair. "I'm waiting to hear what the inspectors have to say. That's going to make a big difference."

Cora became alarmed. "You don't think they'll find Arthur did anything wrong, do you?"

Virgil stirred his coffee. "You don't ever know. Arthur is responsible for everything that goes on in his mine. But he isn't the type to endanger lives for the sake of money."

Scraping his chair back, Earl stood. "Makes me wonder why Cap hadn't already replaced those beams. He had the damn lumber right there. Also, those frames should be inspected every day. I can't help but wonder what happened."

"You know those men have to produce a certain amount of lead and zinc every shift, Earl. First and foremost, mines have to turn a profit."

"That don't mean Art did anything wrong."

"I'm not saying he did."

Earl put on his hat and coat and left out the back door without another word.

She took Virgil's hand. "He's just upset for his friend."

"I understand that. But if the beams were to be replaced, Arthur should've seen it was done. Those men down there depend on the people above ground to take care of them."

"I know. It's awful. Mining is bad for everyone."

"Except those needing work."

LOVE RELEASED

CHAPTER SIX

Virgil took Cora and Jack to Betty's Diner for dinner. Before they finished their meal, the three inspectors came in and approached. Virgil stood and introduced them to Cora. "I thought you'd be eating in Carterville." Virgil leaned closer and whispered. "Anything in here has the potential of keeping you in the toilet all day."

They chuckled and Rydal put his hand on the back of a booth and crossed his ankles. "We already ate, but figured the coffee wouldn't kill us. We checked at the mine again. Ebby noticed a few minor things we took note of."

"Good," Virgil said. "I hope you can get to the bottom of the problem."

Sharpe hiked up his pants by the waistband. "Oh, we know what caused the accident. We just have to figure out who's to blame."

Virgil didn't like anyone coming into his town blaming his people of anything. "I thought this was just an accident. They happen all the time in mines."

"Yeah, but the owner knew there was a problem and he didn't fix it," Ebby said. "Those beams should've been replaced months ago."

Virgil straightened not liking the man's tone. "I'm sure if Mr. Bridges knew there was a problem, he made arrangements to get it fixed. He can't go down in the mines and do repairs himself."

Rydal stepped between them. "We'll have our report in the next couple of days and we'll leave it with you. If there's a problem, the Department of Safety Engineers will decide what to do. We're just here gathering the facts."

The three men moved to the back of the diner and put their heads together. None of that sounded good for Arthur. Virgil knew the man depended on reports from underground about what was happening.

"I'm starving," Jack said. "Can I have a milkshake, too?"

"No," Cora said firmly. "But you can have a glass of milk."

Jack sat back and puckered his lips. "I sure would like a chocolate milkshake."

Cora leaned over and stabbed him with a warning glare. "We can go home and have a Spam sandwich."

Jack's eyes widened. "No, I'll settle for a glass of milk like you said."

She smiled. "Good. I'm glad you came to that decision."

They ate in silence, and before long the three inspectors left to head back to Carterville with a promise to be back early in the morning. That was Sunday and Virgil wasn't going to be in the office, but if they needed him, they knew where to find him.

Back at the house, Cora sent Jack in to take a bath. Virgil put his arms around her and kissed her gently on the cheek. "I'm going over to check on Arthur and see if he's doing okay. No doubt, all this has him pretty shaken up."

"Okay, be careful, the roads are slippery."

Virgil pulled into Arthur's driveway and made his way to the front door. Arthur answered with a glass of whiskey in his hand.

"You have anything to eat before hitting the hard stuff, today?"

"Yes, my cook practically shoved pot roast down my throat. She just left." He held up the glass. "This is my first. Want one?"

"No, I just finished dinner myself, so I'm good."

"There's probably coffee in the kitchen if you've a mind."

"No, I just came to check on you, see if you're okay and tell you that the town is behind you."

"Right now I think they'd hang me from the Mulberry tree in the city square."

Virgil faked a laugh. "It's not that bad. This will all be behind us before we know it."

"I'm not that confident. Nothing will bring those two boys back."

They went into the living room and Arthur sat in his favorite chair while Virgil eased down at the end of an overstuffed couch.

"I wanted to ask you why Cap didn't replace those timbers sooner."

"That's what everyone wants to know, including me."

"Had he known there was a problem for a while?"

"He didn't say a word to me until several weeks ago. It could've been a month or six weeks. That very day I told Dabney to go to the lumberyard and get whatever was needed to fix the problem."

"But he didn't make the repairs."

"I know that now." Arthur took a long drink. "I thought Cap would get that done the day he mentioned it to me. I checked with Casey at the lumberyard and he told me when the materials were purchased."

"You ask your underground boss why?"

Arthur shook his head. "I haven't had a chance to talk to him yet. I just don't understand. I really trusted Cap." His old friend looked at him with concerned eyes. "I didn't want those three idiots thinking I was trying to threaten Cap into saying anything."

"That's a good idea. Stay away and let them do a clean examination. This way, when you're explaining what went on to the Mining Association you can be perfectly honest."

Arthur leaned his head back and exhaled a hard breath. "I don't want those jackals breathing down my neck."

"No one in the town wants them hanging around."

"They're too dangerous and the minute one man says the word union, there's a riot."

"They've been in control a long time." Virgil leaned forward. "Earl said Ruth came by and was running his mouth."

Arthur swiped his hand through the air. "I can handle someone like that piss-pot. I'm sorry as hell that his son is dead. Nothing could be worse, but he's not going to intimidate me with his threats and bullying tactics."

"He's a mean one, all right."

"That's true, but he's not half the man his daddy was, and I gave him a good ass beating right there on Main Street one day."

Virgil stood and stretched his legs. "That was some years ago. Let's hope it doesn't come to that. I'd like you to let me handle Ollie Ruth. He's hurting pretty bad right now, but that doesn't give him unlimited rights to harass you."

"Earl sent his ass packing. I think he'll stay away."

"Good old, Earl. One can't help but wonder about his past."

"I've known him all my life and there are things you don't want to know."

"I'm sure there are. For now, I'm going back to my family and try to enjoy the rest of the night. If you need me, call."

Virgil left and as his footsteps crunched through the snow, Ollie Ruth jumped out in front of him, nearly knocking him backwards. With the heavy snow, Virgil staggered a bit before grabbing Ruth by the lapels of his coat and shaking him as hard as he could.

"Don't jump out on a lawman like that. It'll get you shot."

Ruth yanked loose. "So, you're on old Arthur's side."

"I'm not taking a side because there are no sides to take. Your son is dead and instead of hanging out here at Arthur's house you should be home with your family."

"My wife's heart is broken."

"Go home, Ruth. Don't make me arrest you."

Ruth stared at him, his mouth twisted, his eyes glistening in the bitter night. "You wouldn't do that to a grieving father."

"I wouldn't want to. But, you'd be surprised at the lengths I'd go to keep Gibbs City safe."

"I ain't hurting nobody."

"Then go home, now."

Virgil watched the grieving man get into his battered old car that was held together with bailing wire and a screwdriver. His heart went out to the Ruths. God only knew what he'd feel if anything happened to Jack. The boy meant the world to him. And that's why Jack wouldn't be going down into some mine. No matter what Virgil had to do, where they had to move to, or how many obstacles stood in his way, Jack would have a better life.

Driving home, Virgil passed Leonard Casey's barbershop that he and his wife had been rebuilding and trying to get their lives back together after the fire. It had been a shame that a man eaten up with greed and envy had put Gibbs City's residents through so much. But, Eddie Summerfield was determined to run Carl and Buford out of business even if that meant he had to burn down the whole town. They'd caught him and he was in jail where he belonged.

Virgil stopped in front of the dry cleaners that Arthur owned. He thought about that crazy Bart who'd tried to kill them all, and Reverend Fuller, who now resided in a mental institution, and all those they lost to influenza.

Through it all Cora had been his guiding light.

The goal he'd been working toward, the person that had a heart so full of love it spilled over everywhere. With absolutely nothing of her own to offer but love and compassion, she'd taken up the fight for little Ronnie.

Thinking of the abused boy had always made Virgil slightly melancholy, but Ronnie was with a wonderful family that loved him and would take care of him. Losing the boy had broken Cora's heart, but she'd been strong enough to let Ronnie go.

She fought valiantly for the colored people in their community, and she had been glad to discover JJ was her cousin.

Her Aunt Rose had a colored child out of wedlock. She, too, had been brave enough to let the boy's father raise him in a segregated state where their relationship would never be allowed.

No doubt Rose had loved JJ's father very much and Thomas Johnson was a well-respected man of his community. Thinking back, Cora had changed so many things he couldn't look around and not feel her presence.

She loved and was loved dearly by the people of Gibbs City. Virgil liked to think she'd made the town a better place to live, and him a better man for falling in love with her while she fought against loving him from the start.

He decided it was time to get back home so he could settle in for the night when he saw Carl hurrying past Grover's Grocery Store, his hands in his pockets. Confused that his old war buddy would be out this late, Virgil wondered if he was back on the bottle.

That would spoil everything.

Virgil pulled up behind him and honked the horn. Carl glanced back then continued walking. Strange that he would do that. Carl darted across the street and continued on his way.

Virgil grew concerned and pulled his car over, blocking Carl's path. He rolled down his window and shouted. "Where's the fire?"

Carl threw up his hands and ran to jump in the passenger side of the vehicle. "Quick, let's get to Ben Welsh's house."

"Why?" Virgil asked.

"I'll tell you on the way. Now step on the gas."

Virgil pulled onto the street and headed toward the Welsh house. "You're as worked up as a washing machine. What's wrong?"

From the dim interior lights, Virgil saw the tightness in Carl's face that pulled of his mouth taut.

"That bastard Warren Hayes is back in town."

The news stunned Virgil and had him speeding down the street. "What the hell does he want?"

"His kid. What else?"

They slid to a stop in front of the two story house on Liberty and jumped from the car. They took the steps two at a time and Virgil rang the doorbell.

Ben answered with his glasses in one hand, the newspaper in the other. "Howdy, Sheriff." He looked to the man standing next to him on the porch. "Carl, how you doing?" Ben reached for his coat on the tree rack next to the door. "You need something from the pharmacy?"

"No, Ben. It's more serious," Virgil said.

Opening the door wider, Ben invited them inside. Virgil took one look around outside before entering the house.

"What's going on?"

"I'm sorry to tell you," Virgil said, "But Warren Hayes, Ronnie's daddy, is back in town."

Just then Susan came down the stairs. "What does he want?"

Carl took off his hat and held it with both hands. "I was just closing up my gas station when he came in for petrol." Carl shuffled his feet. "I was surprised to see him back after the way he'd beat his son and Virgil ran him out of town."

Susan stepped closer, a worried frown on her pretty face. "Maybe he's just passing through."

"No, ma'am. He told me he came to get his son and he'd kill anyone who stood in his way."

"But we've legally adopted Ronnie," Ben said. "He's our son now."

Carl shook his head. "Liquored up, Warren don't see it that way."

Ben glanced up the stairs. "You think he'll come here?"

Virgil said, "I don't know, but I'm going to go looking for him and find out exactly what he intends to do."

"What should we do?" Susan asked. "Ronnie's upstairs sleeping. How can we protect our child if that horrible man comes to our home?"

Virgil looked at Carl. "You have your pistol on you?"

Carl patted his coat. "Got it right here in my pocket."

"Then you stay here and guard the Welsh's house. If that SOB comes around, shoot him. He's been warned to stay away from Ronnie."

"Will do. You can count on me, Virgil."

"I'll come back as soon as I learn anything."

Ben and Susan Welsh clung to each other as Carl removed his coat, hung up his hat and took out his pistol. Virgil could depend on Carl to keep them safe until he tracked down Warren.

Leaving the house, he drove home to tell Cora he'd be tied up until he found Hayes. That was a man Virgil hated. After he'd beaten Ronnie so badly he'd nearly killed the poor boy, Virgil wanted to do the same to old man Hayes, but the badge on his chest wouldn't allow that.

He pulled up at the front of the house, hoping Cora had made a fresh pot of coffee and he could fill up his thermos to keep him warm. He had no way of knowing what tonight would bring.

He opened the door, stomped the snow off his boots on the rug then he looked up.

Warren Hayes held Cora against his body, a revolver pressed against her temple.

CHAPTER SEVEN

Cora forced herself to remain calm and quiet. Waking Jack was the last thing she wanted to happen tonight.

"Come on in, Sheriff," Warren Hayes said. "I was just having a conversation with your nosy wife. The one who caused all my troubles."

Virgil stood at the door, his face a mask of confidence, but she knew he was angry because his gun was beneath his coat and not easy for him to reach.

While he'd gone to check on Arthur, Mr. Hayes had practically knocked down her back door. He'd barged in the house waving a gun, making serious threats.

The minute he entered her house she smelled the liquor on the drunk's breath. Alone and defenseless, there wasn't a single thing she could do to protect her and Jack.

"Release her go," Virgil said calmly. "Let's talk, Warren."

"We got nothing to talk about. You get your ass over to the Welsh's house and fetch me my boy."

Virgil shook his head, his eyes searching her face as if silently asking if she were okay. She slowly nodded. "I can't do that. They've legally adopted Ronnie and now he belongs to them."

Virgil pointed at Mr. Hayes and Cora knew he struggled to control his anger. "You, on the other hand, were told to never come back to my county."

When he'd burst through the door, Mr. Hayes looked like he'd just crawled out of a trash can. His hair stuck up, his clothes were filthy and he stunk to high heaven. Anger oozed from his body and had contorted his unshaven face.

With her back against his chest, she couldn't see him, but she felt the rage vibrating off his body. She hated being near the man because he turned her stomach at the way he'd treated an innocent child.

"I'll do as I please. And ain't no lawman gonna change that."

"It's my job to keep the peace, Warren. You were warned to stop abusing Ronnie."

"That's because this bitch here kept sticking her damn nose where it didn't belong. I should've killed her."

"You being abusive wasn't Cora's fault and all she ever wanted to do was help Ronnie."

"My son didn't need no help. I didn't treat him no worse than my old man treated me. A good whooping don't hurt any kid."

"You nearly killed him."

Mr. Hayes swung the gun to point at Virgil. "That's a damn lie. I never did any such thing." The gun was immediately returned to her temple. "This little know-it-all couldn't mind her own damn business."

"She was only a concerned neighbor."

Mr. Hayes chuckled. "You just wanted an excuse to come sniffing around her skirt tails. You were after her like she was a bitch in heat and don't deny it. You shacking up over here because of Ronnie was a joke. The whole town knows you were both going at it all the time."

"That's a lie. Besides, it was you the town talked about. How mean and brutal you were to a defenseless little boy."

"He's my damn kid and I can do as I please to him."

"I can't let you harm that boy again."

"I can do any damn thing I want with this gun in my hand and you can't stop me." Warren let out a cynical laugh that made her cringe. "I could murder the whole family and not a living soul would even suspect me."

"You're wrong. Carl's protecting the Welshes right now. He knows about your plan to get Ronnie back. The best thing you can do is put the gun down and leave town." Virgil stepped closer. "You haven't hurt anyone, so far. If you do, you'll go to prison."

Cora knew Virgil would never let Mr. Hayes go anywhere freely. No, the hate and bitterness he felt for that man ran deep. He didn't take well to a man that abused a child. And Mr. Hayes had nearly killed Ronnie.

"Who'd believe a damn drunk?"

The sound of a shotgun being cocked slithered through the house. "I would," Earl said. "In a New York minute."

Mr. Hayes' hold tightened. "You get out of here old man."

"You put that gun down or we'll be attending your funeral." Earl moved closer. "Your choice."

"You ain't gonna kill nobody. You ain't got the nerve, you old dried up bastard."

A loud, thundering explosion shook the floor she stood on. Cora screamed and Mr. Hayes slumped to the floor, his right shoulder almost blown off, leaving his arm dangling by raw flesh and tendons.

Jack ran from his room, and in an instant, Cora was in Virgil's arms and Jack clung to Earl's neck. "Oh my God."

Earl was careful to keep Jack's face averted, and Cora was relieved when she saw Maggie's family running toward her house. When they hit the door, Earl handed Jack to Maggie's oldest son and told him to get the boy out of there.

Virgil had removed his coat and discarded it on the floor. "Are you okay?" he asked. He led her to a chair. "Sit down and relax a minute." The next thing she knew, Maggie sat next to her holding her hand, and wiping the blood off her face and clothing.

"What happened here?" Briggs asked. "I heard Earl's shotgun go off and I don't know who jumped the highest, me or Maggie."

Mr. Hayes moaned and clutched his shoulder. Virgil went to the phone and called an ambulance. Then he called the Welsh's house and told Carl everything was under control.

Cora buried her face in her hands, not wanting to look at the blood covering her kitchen. As a doctor, she knew she should help Hayes, but her legs were too shaky to hold her. Instead, she had Earl press a towel to the man's shoulder to staunch the bleeding.

"Warren Hayes came in to the gas station earlier today and told Carl he planned to get Ronnie back."

Briggs looked closer. "That's a damn fool thing to do."

Virgil looked at Earl. "No, his mistake was thinking Earl wouldn't shoot him."

Briggs looked at his neighbor. "I knew one day you'd kill someone with that shotgun."

"I didn't, but I came close."

Virgil slapped Earl on the arm. "I'm glad you came when you did. I'm sure he would've killed Cora."

Frowning down at the blood soaked towel, Earl said, "I doubt he's going to be having much use of that arm in the future."

"Serves him right. Once he's fixed up at the hospital, he's going to jail, and this time he's going to stay there."

Cora heard the ambulance, and after the medics had removed Mr. Hayes, she stood on wobbly legs. The sight before her wasn't as bad as she'd expected. Earl and Briggs were busy cleaning up the evidence.

Virgil helped them. When the stove was clean enough she put on a pot of coffee and picked up a rag to help. Maggie stopped her immediately. "Oh no you don't. A woman in your condition doesn't need to be cleaning up blood."

Earl stopped and looked at her. "What condition?"

Maggie looked at her. "You didn't tell him?"

Cora shook her head.

Earl cocked his head. "What didn't you tell me?"

"I'm going to have a baby."

Earl would've hit the floor if Virgil hadn't grabbed his arm and held him upright. "Well, I'll be," he said softly.

Cora smiled at Virgil. "We just found out."

"A little baby. Now don't that just beat all?"

"It's a long ways off."

"It'll be here before you know it." Earl came over, pulled her to her feet and gave her the most heart-touching hug she'd ever had. He squeezed her tightly against his chest in the most loving embrace she'd ever experienced. Cradling her head in his palm, he whispered in her ear. "I'm so proud of you."

She held him close and enjoyed the feeling of family, love and protection. They slowly broke apart. Earl wiped his eyes, and blew his nose into his handkerchief before reaching out and shaking Virgil's hand. "Thank you."

"You're welcome," Virgil replied, grinning. "But Cora had a little to do with it too."

She ducked her head from the embarrassment. With the kitchen cleaned up and things back in order, Maggie and Briggs left. Cora knew she should feel sorry for Mr. Hayes and concerned about his injuries, but it wasn't in her heart.

The man was a monster.

She sat at the table and Earl poured himself and Virgil the remainder of the coffee.

"So, where you gonna put this new baby?" Earl asked. He put up his hand. "Moving is out of the question. This new baby is going to need me."

"Really," Virgil asked. "And why would he need you?"

Earl puffed out his chest. "I'm his grandpa. I can teach a kid a lot. Who do you think taught Jack how to play the harmonica, whittle, clear brush, use a hammer and other stuff?"

"You've been a wonderful influence on Jack," Cora said. And every word was true. He'd been there for her and Jack when the rest of the town had shunned them and tried to run her and Jack out of town. "Our children will be raised right here in this house that's filled with love."

Virgil leaned back. "We could consider expanding and adding an extra room."

Earl looked around. "I don't know, Virgil. You might have to add two to make it even. You don't want it to look like you just stuck a room on the side of the house."

Virgil scratched his jaw. "That's right. How about if we add a second floor?"

Earl looked up at the ceiling. "I'm not sure about that. You might have to check with Ethan. He's the man with that kind of knowledge."

Cora looked at the two men and smiled. Their love swelled her heart and she could barely contain the emotion welling up. They'd make everything all right. They'd care for her and Jack and their future looked brighter than ever.

As long as crazy men stopped coming into her kitchen threatening her life.

CHAPTER EIGHT

Virgil didn't cotton much to church going, but he did like the new minister, and by the smiling faces of those filling the pews, so did the people of Gibbs City.

Daniel Washburn was a fine looking man who preached love and compassion. He was in his thirties and didn't have a family. His calm, soothing voice assured his flock they were in good hands, but the warning to love thy neighbor or else echoed in his sermon as well.

Afterwards, Cora invited the reverend and several neighbors to lunch. While the women remained busy in the kitchen, the men gathered in the living room waiting to be called to eat.

By the gloomy expression on Arthur's face, Virgil knew he was still concerned over the death of the two miners, and the loss felt by their families.

"We'll be having the chapel services for Terry Watters and Sam Ruth on Monday." Reverend Washburn announced in church, but here in Virgil's house, the man of God showed Arthur an outflowing of compassion. He understood guilt and sorrow.

With his hand on the older man's shoulder, Washburn said, "Mr. Bridges, it's not our place to blame or fault. Leave that to God."

"That's a lot easier said than done."

"Most people struggle with that same thing. When we can't know God's plan, it's hard to step back and let Him take over."

That was the end of Washburn's words of wisdom for the rest of the day as he visited with those gathered. His folks came from Carthage and he had a sister in Miami, Oklahoma. He'd received his calling early and Virgil liked him because this wasn't a judgmental man. He lived what he believed, and trusted his faith. Just the kind of minister Gibbs City needed.

The men sat in the kitchen while the kids took up the living room floor on spread-out newspapers. The women ate off plates on their laps. The conversation was quiet, but occasionally Virgil would hear the shrill voice of Ester Cooper, who was once married to Bart, above the crowd.

While Arthur was a self-made man who'd worked hard all his life, his daughter and granddaughter were given the world on a silver platter. Arthur spoiled them rotten and it showed.

"I don't know if any of you ladies have seen the beautiful clothes at the JC Penney's store in downtown Joplin or not, but they are stunning. The shoes are beautiful." Ester said, nibbling on her sandwich. "You must go."

"I haven't been there," Maggie remarked. "I like to do my shopping right here in Gibbs City. The merchants can use our money just as easily as those in surrounding cities."

Ester put her plate aside and picked up her glass of iced tea. "I don't like to shop here. The selection is too small and I have a more elegant taste. Our colored servant, Eunice, bless her heart, is always complaining about all the clothes I have." She smiled and pressed her hand to her chest. "But, I guess after the awful husband I married, who can blame me for trying to forget."

She broke into tears. Arthur stood, took her by the arm and they prepared to leave. Virgil saw them to the door. Arthur apologized for Ester being so sad. "She's distressed today because it would've been their twentieth anniversary."

Cora came over and took Ester's hand. "I'm sorry, Ester. But, you're a strong woman and you can overcome all this."

Ester dabbed her eyes with a lace hankie. "I'll try, Cora. I take so much of my strength from you. If you can overcome the past, so can I."

Cora smiled. "That's the spirit."

They left and Virgil leaned down and kissed his wife on the nose. "She's going to be all right."

Cora bit her lip. "I hope so. Bart was a horrible man who treated people like trash."

"Well, he's gone now and hopefully none of that kind of trouble is going on in Gibbs City anymore."

As people left, Virgil and Maggie cleaned up and insisted Cora take it easy. Maggie put away the last dish and came over to hug Cora goodbye. Earl stayed for one more piece of pie, after he took care of all the trash.

"So what do you think of the new preacher?" Earl asked. "He seems like a fine gentleman to me."

"He's a helluva lot better than Fuller," Virgil said.

"Hush," Cora scolded. "You don't need to be swearing right from the church." She wiped off the table. "Besides, Charles is a very sick man."

"He's a rotten," Earl started then looked at Jack who had bundled up to go outside play with his friend, "So and so if you asked me."

Cora sat down and kicked off her shoes. Virgil saw how tired she looked after all the company. She needed a nice nap and as soon as their neighbor left, that was exactly what Virgil had in mind. "I wonder why Ruth Potter, the school teacher, didn't come this afternoon?"

Earl looked at Cora. "Did you ask her?"

"I did and she turned white as a ghost."

Earl put his cup down. "I wonder why."

Cora did too, but she didn't want to pry. "Maybe she'll come next time. She might've been tired from her visit to her parents in Joplin."

"They'll get to know each other eventually. The town's too small not to," Earl remarked. "I thought Ester was a little more snotty than usual."

Cora tapped him on the hand. "Virgil and I learned today was her and Bart's twentieth anniversary. I imagine she's feeling a bit down."

"Don't know why she should. The bastard nearly killed you all."

Cora slid Earl a warning glare about his language and it was strong enough for him to drop his gaze. Virgil hid a grin.

"You're right," Cora said. "But she once loved the man. He's the father of her daughter."

"I know," Earl agreed, "But, God, what a rotten person. I don't think they come any worse." He pointed a finger at Virgil. "And don't think it didn't get out what he was doing to his female employees. That alone is enough to shoot him."

Virgil cradled his cup and smiled grimly. "I agree, and when I learned how Cora had hoodwinked him, I have to say I was mighty proud of her."

"No one was happy that day in Judge Garner's chamber," Cora said

Earl's brow wrinkled. "Where is Francis? I didn't see him or Ida at church today."

Virgil shook his head. "I'm not sure, but I think he's busy with Ida's trial. She still murdered her husband and according to the law, she has to be held accountable."

"That's too bad," Earl said. "Ervin Butcher deserved to be shot."

"It's still up to the law. You can't take things into your own hands anymore. The court doesn't hold by that theory in today's world. You have a problem, you have to bring it to the law and let them settle it."

"Well, I'm sure Francis will do all he can to get her off. She does have two daughters to raise and the way Ervin Butcher treated her and his daughters he should've been tarred and feathered."

Virgil shook his head. "That's up to the court system."

Earl left and Virgil took Cora's hand. "Let's take a nap on the couch. Jack's at Maggie's for a while and you look like you're about to drop."

She pressed her hand to her back. "I'm really tired. I didn't think having a small luncheon would wear me out so much."

"I'm sure it's the baby."

She went to the sofa while he turned on the radio and brought a blanket from the bedroom. Soon they were cocooned together and she slept peacefully. Virgil looked down into her face and thought of all the love in his heart for her.

Theirs had been a rocky start, but now he realized it had all been worth the wait. Now if things in town would just settle down so he could spend more time at home, life would be perfect.

Closing his eyes, he drifted off to sleep only to be shaken awake moments later by an excited Jack. "Uncle Virgil come quick. Come quick."

What's the matter?"

Jack grabbed his hand. "Come with me."

Cora mumbled in her sleep and as he got off the couch, Virgil covered her up and kissed her cheek. Jack continued to tug on his arm.

Shaking loose, Virgil said, "Give me a minute to get my coat. Hold your horses. What's wrong anyway?"

"You gotta see. You just gotta see."

Jack and Tommy opened the front door and dashed off the porch. Locking up, Virgil ran to catch up with the youngsters. They ran toward Black Water Creek. "Hold on boys, don't get so far ahead."

"Hurry, Uncle Virgil. You gotta hurry."

After climbing over a small knoll, they pointed down to the creek's edge. "That's a dead body," Jack said. "Tommy touched her and she's ice cold."

CHAPTER NINE

Cora woke to the sound of voices coming from the kitchen and Jack's excited chatter. She rubbed her forehead, wanting them all to go away so she could drift back to sleep. But the noise only grew louder.

When she opened her eyes, she jumped to find Jack standing over her. "We found a dead body."

Cora sat up too quickly and her head spun. Thankfully, she was on the couch. Waiting for the world to right itself, she took Jack by the arm. "What are you talking about?"

Virgil put his arm around Jack. "You shouldn't have woken your Aunt Cora. She's tired."

"I didn't, she just opened her eyes."

"But, you've been hovering over her like a hungry baby bird."

"But, I want her to go see the dead body."

"No," Virgil said firmly. "She will not be going anywhere. Now you and Tommy go to your room and play."

Cora swung her feet off the couch. Virgil was usually very soft spoken to Jack and his firm tone had her staring at him. "What's wrong?"

He sat beside her. "Jack and Tommy were playing down by Black Water Creek earlier today."

She gasped with horror. "I've warned him about that. It's too dangerous in the dead of winter. If one of them fell in they could freeze to death." Throwing the cover aside, she came to her feet, grateful she wasn't dizzy. "I'm going to talk to him."

Virgil took her arm and stopped her. That's when she saw Ethan standing in the kitchen.

"Afternoon, Miss Cora."

She nodded hello. "Ethan."

Rubbing her face, she looking around the room and tried to make sense of everything Jack had said. "What's this about a dead body?"

Virgil took her arm and led her to the kitchen table. "As I was saying, Jack and Tommy were down by the creek this afternoon and stumbled across the body of a dead woman."

Cora covered her mouth and hoped the contents of her stomach stayed put. "Oh, my God."

"I hate that they saw that," Ethan said, softly. "That'll be a hard thing to forget."

"Who?" she asked. "Whose body is it?"

"I don't know if you've met her before, but her name is Hilda Weaver. She's that war bride that Mitch Weaver sent for. She's only been here about six months."

"I did meet her at the hospital once."

"Why was she there?"

"She was with her husband. He'd stepped on a broken Mason jar and needed stitches. She spoke very little English, but they understood each other very well."

"It looks like someone bashed her in the head with a heavy object."

"You're kidding."

"No, but I wish I was."

"That poor woman."

Virgil put his arm around her shoulders. "Ethan and I are going to Mitch's house. We'll either tell him something he never wanted to hear, or we'll be staring into the eyes of a murderer."

Cora was stunned. She'd only taken a short nap and when she woke, the world had changed. "You think he might've done it?"

"I have no idea."

"They were a very loving couple when I saw them."

"Things change. I know Mitch saved up every dime he had to bring her here from Germany and he's always been a decent man. But, in matters like this, no one knows."

He and Ethan walked toward the front door. "Be careful," she called out. "If he killed her he'll have no problem doing the same to the two of you."

After Virgil and Ethan left, Cora put on a fresh pot of coffee and nibbled on a leftover sandwich. Maggie came to get Tommy.

"Can you believe what those two have been up to?" Maggie said. An angry scowl covered her normally pleasant face. "I know a little boy that's getting a whooping."

"I'm not too happy with Jack either. He knows better than to go to the creek this time of the year."

Maggie shivered. "I know it's not deep, but it's practically frozen."

"I think if the current wasn't so fast it would be solid ice."

Maggie folded her arms. "Then they'd be out there ice skating and we'd be worrying about them falling through."

Cora let out a breath. "It's hard raising children today. I worry constantly about what could happen to Jack." She lowered her voice to a whisper. "And now they've both seen a dead body."

"I know, and poor Hilda. Who on earth would want to harm her? She was so sweet and happy to be living in Gibbs City."

"I know. It's horrible."

Maggie took a very unhappy Tommy home and Cora called Jack into the kitchen. Standing him in front of her, she folded her arms and glared. "What do you have to say for yourself?"

"I didn't touch the body."

"That's not what I'm upset about." She pointed her finger at him. "You've been warned several times to stay away from Black Water Creek this time of year. It's too dangerous."

"We didn't go to the creek. We just stood on the hill and looked down."

"Then how did Tommy touch the body?"

"Well," Jack started, obviously finding no way out. "We just went down there to see what it was."

"So you were near the creek."

Jack shrugged his shoulders. "Pal went down there and started barking. I called and called him, but he wouldn't come back. We just wanted to get him, I guess."

"Don't blame Pal. I'm really sad that you chose to disobey me, Jack. Your safety is the most important thing in the world to me. My job is to keep you safe, but if you don't do as I say, then you can get hurt."

"I won't go there again, I promise."

"That's not good enough, young man." She stood. "Tonight there will be no radio program and you'll go to bed directly after dinner."

He bowed his head and stuck out his bottom lip. "Yes, ma'am."

"And you can't go to Tommy's for one week."

His bottom lips puckered. "But, that not fair."

"I'm a parent. I don't have to be fair. I want you to stop and think before you do anything else I've told you not to do."

Jack scowled as he stomped off to his room and closed the door. He was angry, but she shook inside. What if he'd fallen in? The person who killed Hilda could've still been in the area and harmed Jack and Tommy. It made her whole body shake and her teeth chatter with fear.

Earl dropped by briefly to see what Virgil had learned about Hilda's death. How the man learned about the murder so quickly she had no idea, and wasn't going to bother asking.

He had a cup of coffee and didn't approve when she told him she'd punished Jack. "Aw, he's just a kid. Let him enjoy life while he can."

Cora's motherly instinct flared. "So you think it's okay for him and Tommy to be in such a dangerous area?"

Earl shook his head. "There ain't nothing dangerous about that little old creek. You can fall in and get wet, if it's winter, you might get cold. But, it ain't gonna kill you."

"But what if they fell in and hit their head and were unconscious and drowned? And Maggie said this year it's very deep because of all the summer rain."

"What if the moon turned green?"

"You're being silly, Earl."

"No, I'm being practical. Boys will always do things they aren't supposed to. That's their nature. It's what makes them strong and healthy."

"Finding a dead body?"

"Now," Earl cocked his head. "How many times is that going to happen in a lifetime?"

"A young boy shouldn't see those things."

"Okay, but he did. You gonna make a big deal about it?"

"Of course I am. I'm his mother."

"'Cause you think if you worry real hard and put enough strings around that boy, nothing's going to happen to him. That's not real life. We all have things happen to us and no matter how many rules we follow, it happens anyway."

"I want him to listen to what I say and behave. That isn't asking too much."

"I'm just saying he's a boy. He's going to do stupid things that upset you. In your condition, you're going to have to let some of that stuff go. I bet you by tomorrow, when he realizes what he saw, Jack's going to be a lot more scared of that memory than he is of you."

She looked at her hands. "I don't want him scared. And I know he saw something that will stay with him the rest of his life."

Earl patted her hand. "Don't be so tough on yourself or Jack. Be grateful the boys are safe."

With that, Earl pushed away from the table to go home. Cora didn't want to talk about dead bodies. "We'll see you at dinner."

"No, I'm eating with Arthur and Ester tonight. Alice is visiting her friend in Joplin still, so I thought I'd stop by and challenge him to a game of chess to get his mind off stuff."

"That's kind of you."

"Whatcha having for dessert?"

She looked at him and smiled. "I don't know yet."

"Well, if it's something good, save me some."

She stood and walked him to the back door. "I always do."

"And don't think too much about Hilda. It could've been an accident. She was a nice lady who didn't have an enemy in the world. I don't think Mitch is capable of hurting her."

"Besides, you just contradicted yourself. If Hilda fell, that proves the river is too dangerous for children. We both know you're only trying to keep me from worrying." She opened the door. "Just so you know, it's not working."

CHAPTER TEN

Virgil pulled up in front of the pretty little Cape Cod home that was well-maintained and showed signs of recent repairs. He looked at Ethan. "This is the toughest part of the job."

"I know. I've been dreading it since I met you on the banks of Black Water Creek."

"Let's see how it goes."

In the late evening chill, Virgil shivered down deeper in his coat. "Man, this has been a helluva weekend. First Warren Hayes comes to the house and threatens to kill Cora, and Jack goes off and finds poor Hilda dead by the creek." They stepped on the porch. "Makes me look forward to Monday."

They knocked and Mitch Weaver answered the door immediately with a concerned look on his face. "What's wrong, Sheriff?"

"Mind if we come in?"

Mitch was a few years older than Virgil. He'd served as an officer in the war since he was a lawyer when he enlisted. Medium height, with chestnut colored hair and mustache, Mitch always wore a black suit. That's why he reminded Virgil of a sheriff in the old west. Rugged, yet decent and upstanding.

Inside the neatly organized house, Mitch's face was pale and dark bags hung beneath his eyes.

"When's the last time you saw your wife?"

"Here," he pointed to the living room. "We had lunch after church today."

"Anything unusual happen?"

Mitch slipped his hands in his pockets. "We got into a little argument. She's been homesick lately."

Virgil put his hands on his hips. "You two not happily married?"

Mitch blinked and looked away. "No we're happy, she just misses her family. I promised her in the summer we'd go for a visit, but she wanted me to move there permanently."

Virgil didn't know if Mitch could even legally do that. "And you said no."

"I told her the government probably wouldn't allow Americans to travel to Germany. Besides, the place is still rebuilding. There are no places to live, very little food, and most of her family is gone."

"So, you argued?"

He shook his head. "No, no, there was no fighting. We just disagreed. Now where is my wife? Is she in trouble?"

Seeing how distraught the man was, Virgil nodded toward the couch. "Let's sit down."

"Dear Lord, don't tell me something has happened to her." He grabbed the front of Virgil's shirt. "Has she been hurt?"

Pulling Mitch's fists free, he backed the man up until his legs hit the couch. Then he sat him down. "I'm afraid we have bad news."

Mitch put the back of his hand to his forehead looking confused. "What's happened?" he asked softly. Then he jumped from the couch and ran for the door. "Where is she? I must get to her. She needs me."

Ethan caught him and held him in a gentle grip. "I'm sorry," Virgil said. "Hilda was found dead this afternoon beside Black Water Creek."

Mitch swung to stare at Virgil. "What? What are you saying?" He spread out his hands. "She was just going to see her friend, Ester Cooper."

"Did she tell you that?"

"No, I just assumed. I figured she'd cry on her friend's shoulder for a few hours and then come home."

"You say they are good friends?"

"Yes, she and Ester were very close. Ester's grandmother was German, so she was familiar enough with the language to communicate. When Hilda came to Gibbs City Ester took her under her wing and they've been like sisters."

"I saw Ester Cooper earlier today and Hilda wasn't with her."

"What happened? How was my wife killed and who would do such a thing?"

"We're trying to find out. It appears someone hit her over the head with a hard object."

Mitch collapsed into the large, overstuffed chair. "But why?"

"It's our job to investigate. Do you mind coming to the station and giving us a statement?"

"I'll do anything to help find out who did this." He stood and put his hands together beneath his chin. "But first, might I see my wife?"

Tears ran down the distraught man's cheeks and Virgil's gut told him this man didn't kill anyone. Now he had to prove it. "Yes, she's in the morgue at the hospital. The Medical Examiner will want to do an autopsy to determine the cause of death."

Mitch moved to the door. If Ethan hadn't grabbed his coat and put it on him, the man would've walked out without any protection from the weather. Virgil had to close the door behind them.

On the way to the hospital, Mitch Weaver cried like a baby. He didn't hold back his emotions at all. Virgil knew if they traded places, he'd be doing the same thing. He quickly sent up a prayer of gratitude that his family was safe.

They entered the morgue and the sight of his wife covered with a white sheet sent Mitch into complete shock. He cried out then collapsed. If Virgil hadn't caught him, he'd have fallen across his wife's body.

Virgil nodded to the ME. "Thank you."

He and Ethan helped Mitch to the car and they drove to the station. Inside, Ethan put on a pot of coffee and Virgil made sure Mitch was as comfortable as he could be under the circumstances.

There was no way he was going to ask the newly widowed man to make a statement. He was too traumatized and practically out of his mind with grief, or he was such a good actor he should have been in Hollywood with the movie stars.

After a cup of coffee, Virgil called Mitch's brother to come fetch him. In minutes, Gilbert thundered through the door, his eyes searching for his brother.

"Hilda's dead." Mitch stood and the men embraced. Since Mitch had heard Virgil, they both cried. Virgil asked Gilbert to take a seat and offered him a cup of coffee, which the man refused. "I never touch the stuff."

"I'm awful sorry to tell you that Hilda's body was found on the banks of the Black Water Creek. When's the last time you saw her?"

"Last night. Mitch and Hilda came over for dinner. We ate then sat in front of the fireplace roasting marshmallows. That's Hilda's favorite thing to do."

"You know of anyone who'd want to hurt her?"

"God, no. Not a living soul." Gilbert's eyebrows pulled closer. "She barely knew anyone. How could a person want to hurt her?"

"Ethan and I will investigate until we find whoever did this. In the meantime, I'm not going to take a statement from Mitch because he's too torn up. Take him home and bring him back tomorrow. Judge Garner is going to want a report at some point."

Gilbert hugged his brother. "You don't think Mitch had anything to do with it, do you?"

"We're not accusing him, but we do have to question him."

"Okay, Sheriff Carter. I'll get him to our folks' house. Then I'll pick him up tomorrow and bring him in."

Virgil held out his hand. "I appreciate that, Gilbert."

Grasping his outstretched hand, Gilbert said, "You're a fair and just man. This town couldn't ask for no better."

After the men left, Ethan walked to the door and looked out. "He didn't kill his wife."

"I don't think so either, but you never know. Two people get to disagreeing, someone gets shoved, a head hits the corner of a table and the next thing you know, there's a dead person."

"That sounds like one of those detective stories," Ethan said. "But, it could've happened that way." Ethan turned and looked at Virgil. "He seems awful disturbed."

"Wouldn't you if you'd just accidently murdered the woman you love?"

Rubbing the back of his neck, Ethan said, "I guess I would."

Letting out a groan, Virgil slumped into his chair. "Just think about it, Ethan. Who else would want Hilda dead? She's harmless and has never bothered anyone."

"What about a war vet who still hates Germans?"

"That's logical. But think about it. We know all the vets in this town and no one's really carrying a grudge that I know of."

"I can't think of anyone right off hand, but that doesn't mean they don't exist."

"We have to look at this from every angle. We'll find who did this and when that happens, they'll go to jail."

Ethan leaned against the wall, folded his arms and crossed his ankles. "We just got rid of an arsonist and now we're looking for a killer."

"We also have a citizen of Gibbs City waiting to stand trial for murder. Who would've ever thought that Ida Butcher would kill her husband in cold blood? I was there that night she emptied a gun into his dead body."

Ethan shook his head. "That's a lot of built up hate."

"I had no idea Ida was suffering," Virgil said. "If I'd known, I'd have put Ervin in jail so fast your head would've spun. But I didn't, so I feel partially to blame."

"None of us knew it was that bad."

"We should've. Our job is to protect the citizens of this county. If they feel they have to kill someone to get justice then we've failed."

"No one would blame either of us, Virgil. We can't go around prying into people's lives."

"I know we can't, but I sure wish I'd have been able to save Ida from all this grief."

"For a town our size, we sure stay busy."

"That's no joke."

Virgil came to his feet and put on his hat. "I'm going home to my family. I suggest you do the same thing. Monday is going to be crazy around here."

"See you. Please try not to call me in the middle of the night with anything else, okay? We deserve a little break from all this."

Virgil grunted. "With the mine cave-in, Warren Hayes, Hilda's murder, and Ida's court case, I'm wondering what the hell's going to happen next."

CHAPTER ELEVEN

Cora had just taken the scalloped potatoes out of the oven when Virgil came through the door looking like something a cat would drag in. She went to him and helped him off with his coat.

"Lord, you look like you've had quite a day."

"I'd say."

"How did Mitch take Hilda's death?"

Virgil shook his head. "Not good at all. He's in bad shape." He hung his hat on the tree stand and followed her into the warm kitchen. "It about tore him to pieces."

"Where is he now? You didn't arrest him did you?"

"No, he's with his family. The man wasn't in any shape to be manhandled by me or anyone else. I'd be shocked if we learn he did it."

"Well," she said, putting her arms around him. "I know you'll get to the bottom of it. You always do."

"I hope you're right."

Earl stuck his head in briefly on the way to Arthur's. "You learn anything, Virgil?"

"Nothing yet."

"You got anything against me telling Arthur? His daughter Ester and Hilda were good friends, she's going to want to know."

"It's all right, Earl. Just don't lead them to believe we know anything because we don't, I swear."

"I believe you. But I can't for the life of me figure out who did something like that."

"Tomorrow I'll open an official investigation."

Earl looked at Cora. "You take it easy. And don't think for one minute I don't smell that peach cobbler baking in the oven."

Earl left and Virgil dropped into a chair at the table, while Cora put dinner on the table. "Where's Jack? I figured he'd have the radio warmed up by now. His program is on in thirty minutes."

"No program tonight."

"What'd he do?" Virgil asked. "Shoot someone?"

"No, he's being punished for disobeying me and playing near the creek. Both boys knew they weren't supposed to be anywhere near it. I've made that clear." she told him. "And he's going to bed right after dinner."

"It scares you, but it doesn't him."

"It's dangerous." The more she said, the angrier she grew. How dare Jack be so reckless with his life? What would she do if anything happened to him? A wave of dizziness washed over her and she grasped the table and nearly fainted with fear.

Virgil grabbed her by the waist and sat her in the chair. For some reason she couldn't hold back the tears anymore and they poured down her cheeks like rain.

"Sweetheart, what's wrong?"

"I'm so scared of losing him. How could he go to that dangerous place and play? What if he fell in? Drowned? Got a concussion?"

Virgil pulled her against his chest and rubbed her back. His loving touch soothed her troubled mind.

"Honey, he's a boy. He won't always do what you or I tell him all the time. He'll make his own mistakes. You're holding on too tight."

She looked at him. "But I love him so much, Virgil. So do you. What if we lost him?" She cried hysterically, and knew it frightened Virgil because he had no idea the thoughts running around in her head.

"He should be punished for not listening, but as a kid, Carl, Ethan and I played down there all our lives. Did we ever get hurt?"

He chuckled, and tilted her face so their eyes met. "We almost broke our necks a time or two, but we learned how to be careful. One time Carl fell in, and because we were so familiar with that creek, we had him out in no time. Snow was ass deep to a giraffe and it was snowing so hard I thought he'd freeze to death before we got him home. But he didn't."

"I don't want Jack to suffer like that."

"Sweetheart, two weeks later we were laughing and bragging about how tough we were."

"You got in trouble, didn't you?"

"My dad said if I went back down there he'd tan my hide."

She wiped her nose, sniffed and grinned. "But you went?"

He grinned. "Damn right. Next chance I had."

"I still want to punish Jack for not listening to me. When it comes to his safety, we have to be in charge."

"Okay, no program tonight, and right to bed."

"I also told him he couldn't play with Tommy after school this week. Maggie agrees. Tommy is in trouble, too."

Virgil looked deep into her eyes, took her hands and squeezed. "I don't agree with that."

She'd been hoping that Virgil would side with her and they'd be united parents. "Why not? Do you think I'm too mean?"

"No, but Tommy and Jack witnessed something very few children ever see. It will stay with them a long time and they need to talk it out. And together is the best way. Kids have a way of dealing with tragic things. They help each other."

Wringing her hands, Cora said, "I can agree to that, if you think it's for the best."

Virgil took her by the shoulders and gazed into her eyes. "I do, and if Jack asks questions about dead people, or dead bodies, or anything like that, we have to be completely honest. Kids can smell a lie."

She nervously chewed her bottom lip. The fear that something bad might happen to Jack wouldn't go away. "Maybe we should start up a conversation with him and Tommy."

Virgil straightened. "I plan to do that tomorrow night after school. I want to give them time to digest what they saw so they'll remember things better."

Stubbornly crossing her arms, Cora said, "Okay, you're the lawman here. You want to tell Jack dinner's ready while I wash my face?"

"I'll also tell him he can see Tommy."

She put her hands on her hips. "Then it will look like I'm mean and you're nice."

"Oh well," he said and disappeared around the corner. So, now Jack would be angry at her, Virgil would become his champion. That wasn't fair but she knew children thought differently than adults and Jack was no exception. A smile curved her lips knowing she could live with that. Besides, she was happy she didn't have to punish Jack any longer.

They enjoyed a peaceful dinner after Virgil had gone easy on Jack. When, after dinner, her nephew asked to go to Tommy's her first instinct was to say no, because she knew he'd go over there and listen to the last of his program. "I'm not too sure."

"I'm really sorry I upset you, Aunt Cora. I won't not do what you say again."

"You do understand that I only want what's best for you and I worry about you being safe? Down by that creek is not safe this time of year. The banks are really slippery and you could slide right into the water."

Jack's face remained subdued. "I know that."

"But tonight you'll stay home and go to bed. We'll see about tomorrow. And I'm holding you to the promise, young man."

"Oh, I promise. After seeing that dead woman, me and Tommy ain't never going back there."

Virgil leaned closer. "Even after you tell all your friends at school?"

Jack hid a smile. "'Pends. If they think it's neat, then I might, but if they get scared, than no, I won't go back ever."

Not quite as unhappy as she expected, Jack went off to bed. Cora turned to Virgil. "I worry about him with a murderer on the loose. Until you find out who killed Hilda, can you check on him and Tommy while they're playing after school?"

"You want me to spy on kids?"

She lifted her chin, came to her feet and turned away. "Absolutely."

He laughed. "Isn't that a little silly?"

"Not at all. If you'd been on their tails this afternoon, they'd have never found a dead body that we all have to deal with."

"I'd have to deal with it one way or another. But I will admit that I wish the boys hadn't seen that."

Just as she poured them a fresh cup of coffee and spooned out the cobbler, someone knocked on the front door."

"Well, we know that's not Earl."

Virgil opened the door and Judge Garner stood on the porch wearing ear muffs, a thick hat and heavy coat. He tipped his hat at Cora. "Good evening."

She stepped back and smiled. "Please come in Judge. We have fresh coffee and dessert."

"I'll take you up on the coffee but pass on the sweets."

Virgil took his coat while he walked into the kitchen and Cora offered him a seat at the table.

"I bet you know why I'm here."

Virgil pulled his coffee closer. "Is it the mine, the murder, or the trial?"

"All three."

"I figured," Virgil replied. "I'd planned to be at your office bright and early in the morning. You kind of saved me the trip."

After taking a sip of his coffee, Francis set down his mug. "No, you'll need to be there anyway."

"Oh?"

"The judge has issued an order that Ida be remanded into the custody of the sheriff in Carthage. They want to move the trial there."

"Why?" Virgil asked, "It happened here and she's a resident of Gibbs City."

"The DA there feels the jury will go too easy on her here since they all grew up together."

"That man doesn't think we'll do the right thing?"

"I guess not."

Cora's heart broke for the judge and poor Ida. The woman had suffered enough at the hands of her abusive husband. "I'm awfully sorry to hear that, but why take her there now? I mean, the least they can do is allow her to stay with her children until she goes to court."

"That's not the way they want it."

Virgil leaned back. "You think they'll sentence her to prison, don't you."

With sad eyes, the judge looked at him. "Yes, yes, I do. And I'm not sure they won't sentence her to death. She killed a man in cold blood."

Cora folded her arms. "She defended herself and her children. A woman has the right to do that."

"Not the way the law sees it."

The thought of a woman being unable to defend herself frustrated Cora and made her want to storm City Hall. "Well, maybe the law and the court system need to be made aware of the fact that women now have the right to vote, and if we can't get some things changed, then maybe we need to be looking at new officials."

"That's some strong talk, Miss Cora," the judge said. "You give those Carthage people the opportunity and they'll throw you in jail just for the hell of it."

"Really, the last time St. Louis tried that, they failed. Maybe it's time Carthage had a taste of the same thing."

Virgil touched her arm. "You're expecting a child. You don't need to be on a picket line."

"Even more the reason I should be. After all, I want my daughters to have just as much justice as my sons."

CHAPTER TWELVE

Virgil wasn't looking forward to being at the office this Monday. With so much going on, there was no way he'd have a peaceful day. He glanced at the ceiling and wondered if someone up there had it out for him. Dropping Jack and Tommy off at school, he drove to the office to find the three mine inspectors waiting for him. "Mornin'," he muttered, heading straight for the coffee pot. "What can I do for you gentlemen today?"

Rydal stepped over with a clipboard in his hand. "We're going back down in the mine today."

"I hope you find what you're looking for."

Ebby scratched his head. "You probably ain't gonna like what we find. It's looking like the owner failed to do the proper repairs to keep the mine safe."

Virgil cleaned out a cup then looked at the three men. "You honestly think there's a way to keep a mine safe?" He shook his head. "Those damn things are all deathtraps and you know it. If it wasn't that men were so desperate for jobs, nobody would work there."

"It's our job to keep them as safe as possible."

"Then why in the hell aren't you making regular inspections like you're supposed to? I haven't seen anyone from your office in over a year."

Rydal raised a brow at Virgil and shoved his friend aside. "You look here. We've got a lot of territory to cover. We're not expected to be everywhere."

"But you always show up after an accident to blame someone. Why don't you let the unions in and let them protect the men?"

All three men practically went blind from their eyes being so big. "There ain't no room for that kind of nonsense," Sharp stated. "Most mines are safe."

Virgil poured scalding coffee into his cup without offering his guests any. "You don't know what's going on until something happens. Then you show up to point a finger, usually at the owner. You charge the owners a hefty fine, then go on to the next problem."

"We're doing our jobs," Sharpe insisted.

Virgil turned his back on the sorry excuses for men, went into his office and sat behind his desk. "Go on and get out of here. Go to the mine and put on a show like you know what the hell you're doing."

"We're the experts on mining safety," Rydal shouted. "We know more about lead and zinc mines than any owner or worker."

"There are no experts and there is no safety."

"If the owner had replaced those beams this wouldn't have happened."

"That's your conclusion? Then why are you going back down? To make it look like you're doing a thorough job?"

"We are doing our jobs. And in this case it looks like the owner failed to keep the mine up to safety standards."

"You know an owner that goes down in those pits?"

The three men mumbled. "Some do," Ebby said. "Not many."

"Most are too damn scared. They depend on their crew chiefs. If you had a damn brain between the three of you, you'd be at the lumberyard checking to see if the timber was bought. If it was, then it's not the owner's fault the work wasn't done."

"Mr. Bridges has a responsibility to make sure the mine was safe," Rydal said. "And he didn't."

"You and I know Cap let him down. But you can't get any money if a worker makes a mistake. You have to hit up the owner."

"We can't just shove the facts aside. Two men were killed."

Virgil, put his cup down. "You think I don't know that? I grew up with most of the miners around here. The whole town knows them. Don't come in my office passing judgment."

"We're laying out the facts."

"You're on a damn witch hunt because you don't know what the hell you're doing." Virgil stood. "Now get out of my office. And when I read that report, if I'm not satisfied, I'll take it to the commissioner myself."

He didn't wait to see if the men followed his instructions, he sat back down in his chair and finished his coffee.

Ethan came in thumbing over his shoulder, he cocked a brow. "I saw those inspectors huffing down the street madder than a hornet's nest."

"They're trying to blame the whole cave-in on Arthur. This way they can slap him with a hefty fine."

"That's the way they operate all over this area. They're nothing but a bunch of money grabbers."

"Yeah, well, they didn't start my day off too good this morning."

Ethan poured a cup of coffee and joined Virgil in his office. "How's Jack?"

"On the way to school. He and Tommy were pretty quiet."

"Hum, I hope they don't start having nightmares."

"We'll have to see. Jack was punished last night for playing near the creek, but Cora was pretty much over it this morning and made sure he got off to school in a good mood."

"That's about all you can do."

"I expect the day to be busy. Judge Garner came to my house last night."

"Oh?"

"It appears Carthage wants Ida to be taken to the jail there until there's a trial."

Ethan's brows pulled together. "That could take months. What about her girls?"

"I don't have all the answers. I sometimes just have to do what I'm told."

"Are they coming to get her or do you want me to deliver her? Should we lock her up?"

"I'm not doing anything until there's a piece of paper giving me strict instructions. The last legal document I saw on the situation said she was remanded into the custody of Judge Garner. And that's how it is until I see different."

"Don't forget about Mitch Weaver," Ethan reminded him. "He's due in today."

"I'm not looking forward to that either."

"Have we heard from the Medical Examiner?"

"Not yet, and I don't expect to until the middle of the week, if not later."

"So, we really don't even know what killed her."

"No, but her head was bashed in pretty good."

"There's the off chance she was choked to death then hit on the head when the killer tried to hide the body down by the creek."

"I didn't see any other marks on her body. There's nothing that would lead me to believe that. Also, there was so little at the scene. Not even drag marks or adult foot prints in the snow."

"I just feel it in my bones," Ethan drained his coffee cup then said, "This is going to be a tough one."

"Lately they all are."

Carl came in and went directly to Virgil's office. "I just wanted to check and make sure your family was all right. I heard Hayes showed up at your house and Earl shot him."

"That's exactly what happened. I'll admit to you both that old Earl can be a thorn in my side, but I was never so happy to see him coming through the back door."

Carl smiled. "I heard he got him with his old shotgun. I didn't figure that damn thing was still working."

"Yes, it is, and he almost destroyed Warren's shoulder with it. I doubt he'll be able to keep his right arm."

"It don't pay to mess with Earl."

"Especially when it comes to Cora and Jack. He's kind of adopted them and is as protective as a momma cougar."

Carl waved then turned to leave. "Just wanted to check on you."

Virgil called out. "Hey, thanks for being there, buddy."

Carl tossed him a salute. "I hope I'm always there when you need me."

After he left, Ethan looked at Virgil. "He's sure made a serious turn around."

"Thank God. I was so worried for him."

"It looks like him and Buford have a pretty good business going."

"Especially with Eddie's closed down."

Ethan ran his fingers through his hair. "Damn, that was the biggest mess I've ever seen. Too bad about his boys. The man ruined his whole family. Tore them apart."

His hands cupping his face, Reverend Washburn peeked through the frosted window of the office. Ethan glanced at Virgil. "What's today, visiting day?"

"Damned if I know."

Ethan opened the door and the young man entered with a smile. "I wanted to let you know that services for the two miners will be held this afternoon at two at the church."

"Thank you, Reverend. We'll be there."

Fiddling with his hat, Washburn looked at Virgil. "I'm a little worried about Ollie Ruth. He's been raising quite a ruckus."

"I've heard. He's kind of a blowhard, but he has the right. He lost a son and by spouting off at the mouth, that's probably his way of dealing with the grief."

"I've tried to counsel him and his wife, but he's so angry and bitter."

"It takes time to get over losing a loved one," Ethan said. "We lost a lot of good people not long ago when the influenza epidemic hit. So, we're all trying our best to get by."

"Do you think you should speak to him before the service, Sheriff?"

"I've tried that. He thinks because Arthur Bridges and I are good friends, I'm taking sides. That's not true, but sometimes you can't reason with Ruth."

"He's threatening violence."

"He knows better than to do anything in my county," Virgil said. "I've kept my eye on him. He can talk all he wants, but he steps out of line, he'll find himself behind bars."

"I think Lyle Watters is taking it as well as can be expected. I spoke to them yesterday afternoon and he and his wife seem to accept the will of God."

Virgil thought Lyle had received the heartbreaking news with unusual calm, and that worried him. When a man loses his son, he should be a little more emotional. Arthur and Lyle had never gotten along since the time Arthur turned him down for a loan to help save their home. Virgil didn't know if that was the reason, but Lyle had resented Arthur ever since.

He and his family moved into town after that, and he hadn't been happy about it. That all happened before the war when money was really tight. Everyone figured Arthur didn't have the money to lend. But, he was viewed as the richest man in town.

"You never know what's going on inside a man, Reverend. But, Ethan and I will be at the funeral just as soon as we finish up with Mitch Weaver."

"I just came from the Weaver family. They're all distraught and confused about who would want to murder a sweet woman like Hilda."

Ethan straightened. "How was Mitch?"

Reverend Washburn shook his head. "He's beside himself with grief."

"Well, it's a horrible thing to happen, especially to a person so young."

"I need to go and make the arrangements," the preacher said. "I'll see you later."

Ethan poured another cup of coffee. "I'm about sick to death of funerals. I figured after the epidemic we'd get a little bit of a break."

"Life goes on and in our business we sometimes have to deal with the worst of things."

After Ethan and Virgil had lunch, Mitch Weaver came in with his brother, Gilbert. From Mitch's unshaven face, his wrinkled clothes and bloodshot eyes, Virgil thought he hadn't had much rest.

"Come on in," Virgil said. "We don't intend to make this any harder than we have to. You've suffered a great loss, but we have to gather all the information we can to find Hilda's killer."

Staring down at the floor, Mitch mumbled, "I understand." He took a deep breath as his shoulders slumped. "I'll tell you everything I know."

Virgil sat down across from him and his brother. Ethan stood behind him.

"You said you and Hilda had a disagreement and she left."

"Yes."

"Was she angry, threatening to leave town, or what?"

"She brought up leaving and going back to Germany. I told her if she wanted to go that badly she could. But I was staying here with my family."

"That made her mad."

"No, I think she was sad and disappointed that I wouldn't do what she wanted."

"What did she say when she walked out the door."

"That she needed a little air and she'd be back later."

"You thought she went to Ester's house to cool off?"

"Yes, I planned to drive over and get her if she didn't come home by dark."

"But you were still there when Ethan and I arrived and it was past eight."

83

"I'd just finished working on some papers when I looked up and noticed the time. I was reaching for my coat when you knocked on the door."

Ethan moved to stand beside Virgil. "Where were you, Gilbert?"

A shocked expression dressed the man's face. "Me?" He thumped his chest then propped his elbow on his knee. "I was at the office, working."

"Anyone see you?"

Gilbert jumped to his feet. "Are you accusing me of killing my sister-in-law?"

Ethan remained calm. "No, I'm just making sure everyone is accounted for during the time of the murder."

"I didn't do it. No one saw me, but I was damn sure there."

"Did you know Hilda wanted to return to Germany?"

"Mitch had mentioned it and our folks threw a fit. They didn't want Mitch to leave again."

"What about you?"

"I didn't have much say in the matter. When he told me, I advised him to give her time and she'd change her mind. I thought she was probably homesick."

Virgil looked at Mitch. "That true?"

"Yeah, my mom got real upset. But they would never harm Hilda to keep me from moving away. I promised them when I came back from the war that I'd never leave home again."

"Okay, well, we'll be in touch. If you remember anything," Virgil said, "let us know."

The two men stood. Mitch touched his desk. "When can I make funeral arrangements?"

"The Medical Examiner will let us know."

They left and Virgil leaned back in his chair. "Are you looking at Gilbert for this?"

"I don't know."

"What would be his motive?"

"Loving his brother's wife."

Virgil thought about that for a moment. Wouldn't be the first time a love triangle went wrong. "That would shake things up."

Ethan looked out the window as the Weaver brothers crossed the street. "In our line of business, you never know who you're dealing with anymore."

CHAPTER THIRTEEN

Cora had a busy day from the minute she stepped into the hospital, until she finally found a moment to grab a quick lunch. Nurse Mae Price sat down beside her. "How's it going today on your ward?"

"We're busy. This is the first time I've sat all day."

"I just finished giving patient Warren Hayes another dose of pain medication."

"It's a terrible thing he had to lose his arm, but I don't blame Earl at all. Mr. Hayes would've killed us without blinking an eye."

"From the way he treated little Ronnie, I'm sure you're right. He's a mean one." She smiled at Cora. "I hear you're expecting."

Cora's cheeks heated. "Yes, and I'm very concerned. I hope everything goes well."

"Why wouldn't it?"

Cora had no intentions of explaining her life story to everyone in town. Enough people knew all ready. "I was told before that I couldn't have children."

"Guess that doctor was wrong." Mae took a sip of her hot chocolate. "You plan to keep working?"

"That's up to Dr. Richie."

"Oh, is he your doctor?" She smiled broadly. "He delivered most of the kids in this town."

"Dr. Lowery recommended him. I like him. He has such an easy manner about him."

"That's for sure. When labor starts and so many things begin happening all at once, he's the calm in the storm."

"I'm glad."

Lowering her head, Mae said. "Well, as a doctor, you're the same way. I swear I don't know how you do it."

"It's not easy sometimes."

Coming to her feet, Mae stood and shoved her chair up to the table. "My break is over. Talk to you later."

"Enjoy the rest of your day."

Cora had a craving for hot chocolate. Heading back to her office from the cafeteria with cup in hand, she ran into Virgil.

She smiled. "Nice seeing you today, handsome."

"I'm on my way to church for the funerals. Thought I'd stop by and see how you're doing."

"I'm fine." She held out her cup. "Want a drink of my hot chocolate?"

He reared back. "No, thanks."

They went to her office and sat down. Virgil propped his ankle on his knee and looked at her. "So, how's Hayes doing?"

"He lost his arm and the surgery to repair the shoulder took over four hours."

"Well, as soon as he's able, I'm putting him behind bars and pressing charges."

She shivered and shoved the drink away. "The memory of him holding that gun to my head just won't go away."

"He's a sick bastard, all right."

"I can't imagine what he was thinking. If I were him I'd be glad my child was being raised in a loving home."

"Hayes isn't that kind of person. He's a bully and only cares about himself."

"I can't say I'm sorry he'll be going to jail. But, it will be awhile before he's released from the hospital."

Virgil came to his feet. "If he gives you any trouble, let me know. I can always transfer him to the medical unit at the Carthage jail. Let them worry about him."

He kissed her goodbye and left her office. She felt bad for Warren Hayes in one way, but in another she felt he'd gotten what he'd deserved. She'd be glad to see him behind locked bars and she was glad that Susan had decided to keep the whole matter a secret from Ronnie. The little boy didn't need to worry about his father taking him away.

She finished her rounds and was headed for Dr. Lowery's office when Dr. Adams stopped her in the hall. "Thanks to you I spent hours in surgery yesterday trying to save a man's life."

She knew Mr. Hayes's injuries were grave, but not necessarily life threatening. "That certainly wasn't my fault. He broke into my house and put a gun to my head."

"Too bad he didn't pull the trigger."

Stunned, Cora watched as Dr. Adams walked past her toward the emergency room. What a horrible thing to say. Her heart thumped loudly in her chest at the thought that he wanted her dead.

When she arrived in Stan's office he must've sensed her concern for he immediately stood and led her to a chair. "Are you okay?"

She didn't want to make the situation worse by getting Stan involved because that would surely send Adams after her. "I'm fine, just a little flushed."

"You should be home resting today after what you went through yesterday. I can't imagine a person insane enough to put a gun to someone's head."

"A man with a gun has appeared in my kitchen twice. And that's two times too many."

"It certainly is." Stan sat behind his desk. "Have you checked on Warren Hayes today?"

"I did briefly. He's Dr. Adam's patient and I didn't want him upset. Besides, I'm not Mr. Hayes' most favorite person."

He rolled his eyes. "I understand completely. James hit me up first thing this morning about being called in to perform the surgery on Mr. Hayes. He acted like it was your fault."

"He was a little bitter when I spoke to him earlier, but nothing serious. I'm sure he'll get over it."

"Don't underestimate him. He's had it out for you since the day you were hired."

"He and Dr. Janson."

"Janson's a strange fella. I've known him for years, but you can't ever figure out what he's thinking. I was surprised when he was made director of the hospital."

Cora knew little about either man. "Why is that?"

"He's not a well-known or admired doctor. We've had several citations because of the way he's handled certain situations that required a delicate touch. The man's like a sledge hammer in a dollhouse."

"Well, I'm aware he doesn't care much for me, but I can live with that. I have before."

Stan tapped his pen against the desk. "I was hoping it would be different here."

"Don't worry. I just wanted to see if you were available to assist me in surgery tomorrow. Mrs. Baker needs her gallbladder removed and I'm not sure we aren't dealing with something more serious. I could use an extra pair of hands and eyes."

He checked his appointment book then looked up at her. "Eight in the morning?"

"That's perfect."

As she left Stan's office one of the nurses approached. "There's a lady waiting to see you in the visitor's lounge, Dr. Carter."

Not expecting anyone, Cora returned a stack of files to her office and made her way to the waiting area. She opened the door and nearly stumbled. Ann Martin, Jack's grandmother sat as stiff as a board. The small, glassed-walled room was as stark as the rest of the hospital. Ann looked strange sitting in the tiny, uncomfortable, lime-green, plastic chairs.

Swallowing her surprise, Cora pushed the door open. "What do you want?"

Ann wore an elegant navy two-piece suit with a small pill box hat and matching purse. Her jewelry was probably Cartier and her hair expertly styled in a short pageboy. She was a picture of sophistication, style...and money.

Strange how dirty cash could hide so many sins.

"I've come to see Jack," Ann replied, her features carefully controlled.

The statement shocked Cora. "Why?"

Ann lifted her chin and sniffed. "He's my grandchild, of course."

"No, he's nothing to you. Remember, you didn't want him."

"That's true. I personally couldn't stand having him around," she said calmly. Then she smiled politely. "Now, I've changed my mind."

An iron fist squeezed Cora's heart. "Why would you decide that now? You can't give him up then come fetch him back."

Clutching her purse in her lap, her mouth tightened. "I certainly can and I will."

"I have legal custody of him. He's mine now and I'd die before ever letting you near him."

"I see you've gone to great lengths. I tried to pick him up from school and the principal refused to let me have my own grandchild."

"There's a reason for that. I don't want you or Dan kidnapping Jack and possibly doing him harm."

Ann stood quickly, her face molted with shock. "How dare you think I'd do such a thing."

Cora came to her feet. "You're capable of most anything, Ann. You've had your fingers in the pie from the very beginning. Just because you got away unscathed doesn't imply you're innocent."

"I've never been accused of a single thing and I never will. I kept away from all that nonsense."

"Really," Cora looked her up and down. "You didn't stay away from the money."

"I have my own money. My father was a wealthy man."

"That money was gone long ago. Everything you're wearing was paid for by prostitutes, dope dealers, and kidnapped children sold into slavery. That's not to mention the illegal booze, the crooked business deals and the buried bodies."

Ann's face twisted in rage. Lunging toward her with a raised hand, Cora reacted without thinking and punched her in the nose, knocking her to the floor. A trickle of blood ran from her nose. Ann appeared stunned for a moment.

Wiping her face with her gloved hand, Ann struggled to her feet. Cora refused to help the woman in anyway. "You forgot where I came from, Ann. I spent five years in prison thanks to your family. Fighting was the first thing I learned."

"You'll go to jail for that."

"You forget who the sheriff is. You can't touch me."

"I have people who can."

"Just try. You can come after me, but remember, if you try to take Jack, I'll kill you myself."

CHAPTER FOURTEEN

Virgil sat in the pew next to Earl who'd delivered the eulogies for both the deceased. He'd known them their whole lives and the families thought it fitting.

As they sang the last hymn, the families were escorted out of the church. The graveside services would have to wait until the ground thawed. In the meantime, the undertaker would keep the remains on ice.

After leaving the church, several people were going to a nearby family member's house for food prepared and donated by friends and neighbors. Virgil and Earl decided to head home. On the way out they shook hands and gave their condolences to the families.

Virgil waited for Ollie Ruth to make a scene, but he kept his mouth shut and his arms crossed tightly. After the services, he didn't stick around, leaving his poor wife to be the courteous one.

Lyle hobbled down the aisle. "What happened?" Earl asked him. "You get hurt?"

"I was splitting logs and dropped a big one on my feet. Smashed my toes good. I reckon I'll be okay in a few days."

Virgil looked down and saw that both his boots were untied. "Maybe you should have a doctor look at that. You might have a broken foot."

"I can't, got too much to take care of right now. Without Terry's money coming in I'm going to have to get back to work."

Virgil hated hearing that. Lyle had worked for years as the janitor for the hospital and school. But, money was tight all over. He wondered if Lyle and his wife had expected their son to support them the rest of their lives. Terry had been old enough to have a family of his own.

"Looks like Reverend Washburn might fit in nicely with the citizens of Gibbs City. It's kind of sad he had to preside over a funeral only a week after arriving, but I guess there wasn't anything we could to do prevent that."

Looking around, Earl said, "Nice turn out for the weather being so shitty."

"You better watch your mouth. You're standing in a house of God."

Earl looked up. "Well, if He ain't heard more than that, He's not doing his job."

"Cora would box your ears," Virgil teased. "Probably wash your mouth out with soap or send you home without supper."

Earl chuckled. "I bet she would."

As they headed toward the open double doors Virgil glanced outside. "Looks like more snow. Guess we don't have to worry about a white Christmas."

"You're right. It looks like we're going to have more snow than we know what to do with."

Ethan came up and shook hands with Earl. "I'm heading back to the office for a bit. I want to see if anything came in. We've not heard from Carthage yet."

"Well, I'll be damned if we're going to deliver a detainee without the paperwork."

Ethan left and Earl slapped Virgil on the arm. "Cora will pop you for cussing, too."

"Let's just not mention it, shall we?"

Earl laughed good-naturedly. "I'm glad Arthur came to the funeral even though there was the possibility he might've been sitting on a powder keg."

"I'm just glad nothing happened. There's no place at a funeral for an argument. I have to say, I half expected Ruth to jump up and start shouting all kinds of crap."

Earl buttoned his coat. "I'm surprised he didn't."

"It's not that he doesn't have the right to be angry because his son is dead, but he can't blame Arthur."

"You're right, Virgil. But he damn sure should've blamed that lazy assed, Cap. I don't need no damn report to tell me that man wasn't doing his job. He had no reason not to have made those repairs. He's been a miner most of his life. He knows how important those things are." Earl straightened his hat as they exited the church. "Nothing I hate more than a careless or lazy miner. They get people killed."

"I've been thinking about that myself. Wonder if the inspectors talked to him?"

Earl shook his head. "Those men couldn't find their asses in a hail storm. They don't know a damn thing about mining." He harrumphed. "Call themselves engineers. Hell, you can't learn the mood or the character of a mine in no school. They can be as temperamental as a loose woman and the Lucky Lady has been trouble from the beginning."

"I knew she had some problems when I was a kid, but no one was ever killed."

"That's a mine for you."

"That was an accident clean and simple. I haven't read their findings yet, but if they go after Arthur, I'll file my own damn report."

Through slanted eyes, Earl looked at Virgil. "They go after Arthur, you let me know and I'll fix them."

Earl got in the squad car beside Virgil and they left to pick Jack and Tommy up from school. The boys would stay with Earl until Maggie retuned from paying her respects to the families and dropping off food she and Cora had made the night before. Maggie didn't plan to stay very long, and Earl didn't mind the boys playing at his house when Virgil had to work late and Cora was still at the hospital.

Virgil wanted to laugh but he didn't dare. Hell, he had no idea what his neighbor was capable of. One thing for sure, Earl knew exactly where to put that bullet in Hayes's arm to keep from hurting Cora and killing Hayes. Few people in the world can do that. Virgil only knew one other and he was buried in Normandy.

When they pulled up to the school, the bell rang, and the boys ran down the steps to the car and jumped inside, happy to see Earl. "Howdy, Uncle Earl," Jack called out. "Whatcha doing today?"

Earl sat in the front seat, but turned around to smile at Jack and Tommy. "It appears I'm stuck with the likes of you two rascals until suppertime."

"Good," Tommy said. "You can tell us one of your stories again."

"Stories?" Virgil asked. "What stories?"

Earl nudged him on the shoulder and winked. "You know, all about my exciting life as a spy."

Virgil grinned. That would keep the boys interested for sure. Now, if Earl put on a costume with a red cape, and S on his chest and fly, they'd be really happy.

Stopping in front of Earl's house, Virgil let everyone out. The boys were excited and Earl corralled them into his yard and up the steps. Virgil smiled as he backed up and headed toward the office.

He was more anxious than usual. There was just too much going on for such a small town. He'd yet to hear from Carthage about Ida, there was no report from the mine investigation, and no results from the ME yet. As he made his way through the snow, he hoped this wouldn't be another day of waiting.

Ethan's pickup stopped in front of the station just as Virgil drove up. Outside, standing in the cold, Cora waited. She didn't look happy.

Jumping from his vehicle, he ran toward her and grabbed her by the arms. She was white as a sheet. "What's happened?"

"Ann Martin came to the hospital today. She went to school and tried to get Jack out of class."

He opened the door and escorted her into his office. Ethan knew pretty much everything, so he didn't bother closing his door. Easing her into a chair, he took her purse and hat and placed them on a nearby table.

He sat on the corner of his desk. "Who's Ann Martin?"

"That's Dan's mother. You saw her in court."

Fear crawled up his spine like a spider making him shiver. "And she came to get Jack?"

Cora nodded.

Virgil alerted Ethan. "Get on the phone and call Earl. Tell him not to let the boys out and don't let anyone in."

"I'm on it."

Cora wiped tears from her eyes with a shaky hand. "She just showed up out of the blue."

"That's because Dan's been told to stay out of Gibbs City, so the coward sent his mother."

"Remember us talking about her being behind him wanting Jack in the first place?"

"I do." He took her hand. "I never thought she'd come here and try to take the boy."

"Can we stop her?"

"I'll check with the judge, but you know what JJ said. You've been granted custody of Jack, but we've never adopted him."

"I know there is a difference, but I didn't think they'd bother us. They didn't want him before." Virgil handed her his handkerchief and she dabbed her eyes. "After Eleanor was murdered the Martin's practically threw him on my parents' doorstep and drove away. What's changed?"

"Well, my guess is like we said before, she's out to hurt you and this is the only way left."

"But, she'd also be hurting her own blood."

"I don't think that family thinks like that. Jack would just be a trophy for them to gloat over. Something they could smear in your face."

She hugged herself and rocked back and forth. "God forgive me, but I hate those people."

He tilted her face up and gazed into her eyes. "We need to see about adopting Jack and making it legal so we don't have these kinds of problems."

She stood and grabbed his shirt. "But Virgil, what about my past? One hint of me being in prison and no judge would allow me to adopt."

Virgil grinned. "I know one who would." He pulled her into his arms and kissed the top of her head. "We've had everything in the world thrown at us and we're still a family and still happy. Let's go home."

He instructed Ethan to let him know if he heard anything, and he and Cora walked out the door. From across the street, Ann Martin walked out of the courthouse, a smug expression on her face. She tipped her nose arrogantly and slid into a brand new Cadillac with a colored driver.

"She looks pretty confident."

Cora lowered her head and bit her bottom lip. "She's probably been to see the judge."

He looked at her. "Why?"

"I punched her in the nose."

CHAPTER FIFTEEN

Cora lowered her gaze and wished she'd given her actions a second thought before striking out.

Virgil leaned down and tilted his head. "What did you say?"

"I hit her. I'm sorry," she gritted out. "I lost my temper."

Virgil looked at the courthouse. "I'd say."

"She raised her hand first."

"But you assaulted her. That's against the law, Cora."

She wrung her knitted gloves. "I know that."

"Then why did you do it?"

Anger churned her stomach. "I just got mad. So mad I wanted to punch her."

"That's certainly not like you at all. You are usually against that kind of violence. If a person came up and told me you hurt someone I wouldn't believe them."

"I'm sorry now," she muttered. And she truly did regret hitting the woman. However, she'd do anything to keep Jack safe with her, no matter the cost. "I wish I'd exercised more control."

Virgil put his arm around her and helped her to the car. "Let's get you home. If she filed charges, we'll know soon enough."

They drove home in silence. Cora felt horrible and was ashamed of her unprofessional behavior. What if her actions got Jack taken away? Then where would she be?

When they entered the kitchen, Earl sat at the table watching the boys play a game of checkers. Pal was in Earl's lap, benefitting from Earl's attention. "Glad to see you made it home. A storm is coming."

Virgil removed his coat. "I'm glad we made it home before it hit. It's been miserable all day."

"I'm glad Maggie made chili for supper tonight and she's agreed to share." Cora put her coat up and reached for an apron. "I'll mix up a batch of cornbread."

Before Cora put the pan in the oven, Maggie dropped off a large bowl of chili and took Tommy home with her. They sat down to a meal of fragrant cornbread and chili.

"You find out anything today?" Earl asked, crumbling crackers in his bowl. He gave Jack a careful look. "About you know what?"

"Nothing yet. Ethan's sticking around the office for a while should something come in."

Earl picked up his spoon. "Jack's become quite the checker player. Beats Tommy nearly every time."

"That's good," Virgil said."

Cora knew he was upset because she'd hit Jack's grandmother, but he had no idea how angry the woman had made her. Now, she knew he waited on pins and needles for the judge to call him about the incident.

She wanted to apologize again, but it was useless, because she couldn't undo her actions. Hopefully, the judge wouldn't throw the book at her, even though she deserved it.

After dinner, she turned on the radio so Jack could listen to his program and curl up with Pal. That seemed to be the most relaxing for him. She picked up the pot and filled everyone's cup to go with dessert.

"You may as well know I made an idiotic mistake today, Earl," she said. "Jack's grandmother came to the hospital this afternoon."

Her neighbor's face turned stormy. "What's she doing hanging around here?"

"Keep your voice down," Virgil warned. "I don't want Jack upset."

"She came to take him out of school, but when they wouldn't release him, she came to the hospital."

"You tell her to get out of town?"

"No, I punched her in the nose."

Earl barked a laugh. "Hell, that's even better."

"Probably not to the judge," Virgil said. "We saw her coming out of the courthouse."

"That don't mean squat. Francis is a reasonable man. He'll make the right decision."

Cora shoved back her chair. "Like arrest me for assault."

Earl shook his head. "He's not going to do that. I doubt he even mentions it."

"Oh, I wouldn't count on that," Virgil said. "Cora assaulted a woman and the judge doesn't take kindly to that kind of behavior."

"What's he gonna do? Lock her up?"

"He could."

Earl shoved his plate aside. "Over my damn dead body, he will."

"You're not the law in this town, Earl. I am. And I don't mind saying that Cora should've exercised a little more self-control."

Swiping away tears, Cora replied, "I wish I had as well."

Earl chuckled. "I bet Jack's grandmother does too."

Virgil's lips tightened. "We'll be lucky we don't lose Jack."

Earl stilled, his stare shocked and unbelieving. "Why would that happen?"

"I should've shown more restraint."

"That's hogwash and ain't nobody in this town going to agree with that. I'll talk to Francis myself."

Virgil raised his hand. "Let me handle this." He looked at Cora. "She's my wife."

"I can't believe she just hauled off and cold-cocked someone."

Cora leaned closer and lowered her voice. "She came after Jack."

"You live here and she doesn't," Earl reminded her. "Folks are more likely to believe you did the right thing."

Even now, Cora didn't know what to think. Hitting Ann had been wrong, but not wrong enough for her to lose Jack. She busied herself around the kitchen until time for Jack to get ready for bed. Earl had lingered over an extra cup of coffee when she went into the bathroom to draw a tub of bathwater.

Arthur's voice carried from the front of the house and she went to investigate. Standing in the hallway she thought the older man sounded frantic. Had something happened with the mine again?

Entering the room, she found Virgil slipping on his jacket. Her neighbor right behind him. "What's going on?"

Arthur stood between Earl and Virgil. "Ester hasn't come home. I don't know where she is."

Dread clutched her heart in a tight grasp. "Where did she go?"

"I thought she'd gone to her friend's in Joplin. Alice was already there visiting the friend's daughter. I knew Ester was kind of blue and thought she'd gone there to get away."

"She's not there?"

"No, Alice called me a few minutes ago to see when her mother was coming to pick her up."

"Oh dear." Cora looked frantically at Virgil and Earl. "She was here yesterday afternoon for lunch with the reverend."

"That's the last I saw her," Arthur said. "She's been missing since then."

Aching for the older man, Cora touched his arm. "We'll find her. Please, don't worry. Take off your coat and let me make you some warm cocoa."

"I need to go with them."

"No, it's best you wait right here. I'll call the operator and tell her that if Ester calls your house to transfer her here."

Exhaustion deepened the wrinkles in Arthur's face.

Virgil opened the door. "Cora's right. I'm going to get Ethan and we'll start looking right away. My guess is she's with a friend."

"What if she did something foolish?" Arthur looked away. "I couldn't live with myself if she came to any harm. She's all I have. She and Alice are my life."

"Let's just be calm," Cora said softly, helping Arthur off with his coat. "You're half frozen already. You wait here with me." She turned and nodded to Virgil. "We'll know as soon as they find out anything."

Weary, Arthur slumped into the chair, and propped his head on his hand. "I can't understand. She's already been gone a whole day. What if she's in danger, her car broke down." He glanced out the window. "The weather's turning worse, too."

She took his hand in hers. "We can come up with a lot of horrible what ifs, but let's stay positive until something happens to change that.

She put milk, cocoa and sugar in a pan. It smelled delicious and made her mouth water. Jack came out of the bathroom with a towel wrapped around him. She hurriedly put his Superman pajamas on him and sat him at the table with a cup of warm cocoa next to Arthur. While Jack chatted, Cora quickly and as quietly as possible called the reverend. If there was anything wrong, they'd need all the help they could get.

Finally wound down, Jack yawned after emptying his mug. Wiping the chocolate mustache off the boy's face, Cora tucked him into bed. As gently as possible she assured him that there wasn't anything wrong and everything would be just fine.

After she'd been sitting at the table for a while with Arthur, the reverend came and spoke with her friend. Reverend Washburn was a good man and right now, Arthur needed someone besides her assuring him that everything would be all right.

"I remember your daughter quite well, Arthur. She's delightful. You mentioned your granddaughter was in Joplin visiting her friend."

"Yes, Ester grew up with Mary and when she married they moved away, but the two remained close. They both had daughters who became friends."

"Well, that's wonderful."

Arthur looked away. "I worry that Ester's out there in the cold."

"Don't allow your mind to go there. Let's pray the Lord is looking over her."

Arthur slapped the table. "I just can't imagine what's happened to her. Where'd she go?"

"Have you tried calling all her friends?"

"Yes, I phoned every one of them and they assured me they hadn't laid eyes on her recently. Even Mary said she hadn't heard a word from Ester."

"I'm sure Sheriff Carter and the Deputy will find your daughter and bring her home safe and sound."

"This has been the worst week of my life."

"I understand," the reverend said, "But God is always with us."

"I hope he's with Ester."

"We have to keep our faith."

Arthur looked at Cora. "What do you think has happened?"

"I have no idea, but Ester would never willingly go away for a day and not let you know where she was if she could."

"You're absolutely right."

Cora held up her hands. "But, let's be patient until we hear from Virgil."

"Yes," the reverend said. "They may have good news."

Cora liked the reverend and hoped he told the truth, but she had a feeling Ester had somehow gotten herself into a situation where she couldn't contact her father and that was serious.

CHAPTER SIXTEEN

Virgil and Earl rounded up as many people as they could and asked them to report to the Sheriff's office right away. When they returned, Briggs, Judge Garner, Ethan, Carl, Frank, Buford and JJ waited for them.

"I don't want to alarm anyone, but Arthur Bridges hasn't heard from or seen his daughter since yesterday afternoon. All of the inquiries have come up empty. So, I need your help."

JJ stuck his hands in his pocket. "We're more than happy to help. Just tell us what to do."

"You and Buford search your community. You know it best. Frank, you and Carl take the west side of town. Ethan, you and Briggs go east. Judge Garner, you and Earl go south and I'll go north."

Frank the fireman stepped forward. "Exactly what are we looking for?"

"Hopefully her car. Let's hope she's not out in this weather. That could spell bad news for her." Virgil took his shotgun down off the rack. "Arthur has called all her friends as well as those who might know Ester's whereabouts. So, our job is to comb the town and try to find her. We'll lay it out like a grid and search every street, alley and deserted building."

Carl headed for the door. "We all have cars but we can't stay out in this weather long."

"I know," Virgil said. "Meet back here at my office in two hours. Then we'll regroup. If you find her, bring her here and call my home immediately. Her father is waiting for word."

As everyone filed out of the office, Virgil didn't hold a lot of hope they'd find anything because of the weather. Snow came down so thick he could barely see the courthouse from his office.

Not willing to let anything stand in his way, he climbed into his car and began tracing the neighborhoods and those areas close to his house. If she was last seen there, where would she go?

He'd been out about an hour when he saw Lyle Watters walking near his home. He looked to be in a hurry even with his limp. Curious, Virgil pulled over beside him. "Evening, Lyle."

"Howdy, Sheriff."

"What you doing out this late in a snow storm."

Lyle looked at him and leaned his head inside the car. "I had to meet with the undertaker for the final arrangement of Terry's burial."

"This time of night?"

"I'd been waiting, hoping Mr. Bridges would offer to pay for everything. But he's holding off until the inspectors have their say."

"That's pretty usual."

"Yeah, but Mr. Buckley wants his money."

"Do you have it?"

"I don't know."

Virgil had never known Buckley to demand money from anyone. Usually he had to wait to get paid by the insurance companies. Few people in Gibbs City had cash on hand for a burial.

"Have you seen Ester Cooper? She's come up missing."

Lyle leaned back, his eyes darting around. "Out here in this storm?"

"Last she was seen was yesterday."

"I ain't seen nothing at all." Lyle flipped up the collar of his coat and stepped back to the sidewalk. "I'll let you know if I do."

Virgil continued on the street, watching Lyle in the rearview mirror. Something wasn't right. The streets were deserted and Lyle was out making financial arrangement for his son's burial. Couldn't that wait until tomorrow?

After another hour of seeing nothing but snow pile up, Virgil headed back the office. The judge and Earl were already there having a cup of coffee.

"You find anything?" Earl asked. "Anything at all?"

"Nothing." Taking a cup of coffee, Virgil blew on the brew before finally braving a sip. It scalded his tongue.

"Be careful, that's hot," Virgil said.

"It always is."

"What do we do now?" Judge Garner asked. "The weather is getting worse."

"I know but I hate to go back and tell Arthur we don't have anything."

"You might not have a choice."

Slowly, the men returned to the office, all empty handed. Soon, JJ and Buford left and went home with a promise to keep an eye out the following day when they could see something besides snow.

After they left, Briggs, the judge and Frank called it a night. Earl, Ethan and Virgil stood in the office, Virgil wondering how he'd tell his friend he'd let him down.

"I can't think of a place we've missed," Ethan said. "Not in the town limits."

"We checked all the abandoned mines for any signs of visitors," Earl said. "There were no tire tracks, footprints or anything else out of place."

Virgil put his cup down. "We know all the places we've looked, where we've not checked?"

Pulling down his hat, Ethan said, "I checked every single abandoned building. I didn't see anything."

Virgil looked at the men. "Anyone check Black Water Creek?"

Earl lowered his eyes. "I don't want to think about that."

"Me either," Ethan agreed. "Hilda was murdered down there. I hope and pray the same thing didn't happen to Ester."

"If it has, we have a more serious problem on our hands than we anticipated."

Ethan stood. "Let's go check it out."

"Yeah," Earl said. "Let's not beat around the bush. Better we know what we're up against."

They all bundled up and piled in Virgil's squad car. He'd contacted Cora to let her know they were still looking.

The disappointment that he hadn't found anything echoed in her voice. "Please, try to find her, Virgil."

"I'm doing my best." He slipped on his hat. "I'll be home as soon as I can."

They drove out to the edge of town where the creek curved into the southern part of the town. There wasn't much around there because right before the war the area flooded, destroying several homes. No one had bothered to rebuild there again. Now, it was a little more than a stream with a high embankment.

It didn't flow all the way through town, it came to a bend creating an area where people sometimes fished and kids played around when they got bored. The place wasn't a pretty sight because very little vegetation covered the banks and most of the time it was icy in the winter and muddy in the summer.

Parking near the riverbank, they stepped out of the car with flashlights and began to search the area about a mile from where Hilda Weaver's body had been found. Working their way to the murder site, they slowly covered the distance looking for any hint of Ester's whereabouts.

There didn't seem to be much as they looked along the banks. Getting as close as they dared to the water, they couldn't make out much. As Virgil stepped closer, he slipped and almost went sliding into the nearly frozen water.

"It's too dangerous for us to be out here this late in a snowstorm," Earl said. "Let's call it a night and start over first thing in the morning."

Virgil and Ethan agreed and the daunting thought of having to tell Arthur the bad news clawed at Virgil's heart. He swept the area one more time with his flashlight hoping for a miracle. He hated to hurt the man.

As Ethan rounded the back of his car, Virgil called out, "Hey, there's something up there."

Ethan and Earl followed him with their flashlights shining the way.

"What did you see?" Earl asked. The bottom of his face tucked down inside his coat. "Was it moving?"

"No," Virgil said, squinting into the distance. "It was a color of some kind. Like red."

"Ester's car is red," Ethan said and the man moved quicker toward the unknown object. "Could that be what you saw?"

"Maybe."

Darkness surrounded them and blowing snow had them locking arms so they wouldn't lose track of each other. Crystals sharp as glass shards blew against Virgil's face and stung his eyes, but he continued.

Snow covered his boots and their passage was slow and deliberate. They had to be careful because the creek took a dangerous turn up ahead. One wrong move and they'd be in the frigid water.

Heads down, the men forged ahead. Virgil didn't think they were making any progress and he worried it all might have been his imagination or wishful thinking.

"You see anything yet, Ethan?"

"No, nothing but this damn snow."

"This is like being in a white tornado," Earl griped. "I'm not sure we can find anything."

"Let's go just a little further. If we don't see anything we'll head back." They pointed their flashlights ahead but the snow made visibility difficult.

"What would she or her car be doing out this far? Nobody messes around here. The place is isolated. Since the flood most people stay away."

Virgil didn't want to say anything but his gut told him this was a perfect place to commit a murder. The area was isolated and too rough even for fishermen. At least one person had found it useful.

He couldn't see or hear a thing. Virgil hated to admit it, but if Jack and Tommy hadn't been playing around Black Water Creek they would've never found Hilda's body until spring.

Trudging on, his toes frozen, his face numb and his fingers like ice, Virgil was just about to abort the mission when he caught another glimmer of something and it was red. "Up ahead, men. There's something there."

"I see it, too," Ethan said. "Can't tell what it is, but..."

Just then the three men walked into a hard object. Virgil brushed away the snow with his gloved hand and shined his light. It was a car.

"Quick, Earl, see if anyone is inside."

Ethan and Virgil traced the car, trying to find exactly which way it pointed. He heard Earl pull open the car door and asked, "Anyone inside?"

"Not a soul," Earl called out. "But I found this."

Virgil looked toward Earl's voice but couldn't see anything and that included his neighbor. "What is it?"

"Looks like Ester's pocketbook."

CHAPTER SEVENTEEN

Cora had put on fresh coffee and took out some cookies she'd baked the other day. Not sure what to do, she tried to putter around the kitchen, hoping Virgil would come through the door any minute with good news.

The new minister stayed while they waited. It appeared the preacher's words and compassion gave Arthur comfort. She was relieved because she had no words for times like this. Times a soul hurt so badly there was nothing to make it better.

She'd just turned from the sink when Virgil and Earl came in the back door, both covered in snow and ice crystals. They brushed off most of the snow, and hung their coats out on the back porch to thaw. Stepping out of their boots, they padded into the kitchen.

Arthur jumped to his feet. "Did you find anything?"

Virgil handed Cora a purse. She laid it on the table. "Is that Ester's?"

Arthur took the snow covered red clutch and looked inside. Taking out several items he nodded. "Yes, this belongs to my daughter. Where did you find it?"

"It was in her car, not far from the bend in Black Water Creek."

Arthur paled, and Cora hurried to get her husband and Earl something warm inside them to chase away the chill. They looked exhausted and practically frozen.

"Earl, you have no business out in this kind of weather," Cora complained. "You'll come down with pneumonia."

Fussing, she handed them towels to dry off before wrapping light wool blankets around the two men's shoulders. She clutched Virgil's hand and found it ice cold.

"Was Ester there?"

"We looked all around the vehicle. We covered the nearby area, but we couldn't see a thing. There's just too much snow flying around."

"What would she be doing way out there?"

"I don't know, but I'll find out more tomorrow." Virgil glanced out the darkened kitchen window. "Maybe we can see something when daylight comes."

"I'll go with you," the preacher said. "I'll help search."

"I will too," Arthur said. "At least now we have a lead."

"We'll have to canvass the entire area and see if there are signs of a struggle or if she met someone and drove off with them."

"If she did that," Arthur said, "She would've called me." He turned his keen eyes on Virgil. "Were there signs of a struggle? Was she dragged from the car?"

Virgil and Earl shared a look. "We didn't see that. But, it's impossible to make anything out in this weather. We'll know more tomorrow."

Cora's sympathy went out to Arthur. No doubt his heart ached with concern and agony not knowing where his only child was. She couldn't help but feel there were things Virgil wasn't saying. Perhaps he wanted to keep Arthur from falling apart.

"I'll be up early and meet you there."

"Don't touch anything. If there is foul play, we'll need all the evidence we can get."

Arthur sat up straight. "You don't think Ester met with the same fate as Hilda, do you?"

"Let's not think like that," Virgil said. "That would be unthinkable, but we have to keep an open mind. Right now, we're dealing with a missing person and that's the way it's going to be until I know otherwise." He held up his hand. "There could be a simple explanation. We just have to wait and see."

Earl left. No doubt he was exhausted and Cora hoped he'd skip tomorrow. Knowing him, he'd be right in the thick of things. Arthur and the reverend went to their respective homes, leaving her and Virgil alone.

"So what do you think happened?" she asked, rubbing his cold hands. "Has she been murdered too?"

"I don't know much, Cora." He gripped her hands and worry lines creased his brow. "It doesn't look good. Ester had no reason to be way out there. With the car not two miles from where Hilda was found, it makes me wonder."

"Do we have someone running around town killing women?"

"I don't know. I bet somehow these cases are connected. I just haven't figured out how yet."

"Who in town would do such a thing?"

He shook his head. "I plain don't know."

She stood and went to the bathroom to run a warm bath for Virgil. He'd need to warm up before bed. She didn't want him coming down sick.

She came out to find him standing in the doorway to Jack's bedroom. "I look at him and I'm so grateful he's safe."

She wrapped her arm around his waist. "I feel the same way. That's why my heart hurts so badly for Arthur."

"You never stop loving them."

"No, they're yours forever."

He took her in his arms and squeezed her tightly against his chilled body. "And we have a new addition to look forward to."

Cora thought of her unborn child and wondered how their lives would change after the birth. How would Jack take to his new cousin? And since they'd never discussed having children, she wondered if Virgil really wanted this child.

They slipped apart when she realized the water was still running. "Oh, I'm going to flood the house."

He went into the bathroom, undressed then settled into the tub. As he leaned back, Cora knew how weary he must feel. No one in the area worked harder than her husband. The residents didn't know how lucky they were. She went into the kitchen to mop up the melted snow from Virgil and Earl's boots then put her nightgown on and went to bed.

Soon Virgil joined her, his body still warm from the bath. "You're cold," he said, cuddling up next to her. "Come here so I can warm you up."

She pressed against him and put her hand on his chest. "I'm worried about Ester." She shifted closer. "You think something has happened to her, don't you?"

"It's not looking good. There was no reason for her car to be way out there. And it appears there isn't anything wrong with the vehicle. We didn't move it because I want to study the crime scene first." He stopped and cleared his throat. "I mean the area in the daylight."

Rising on her elbow, she asked. "Do you think she was murdered like Hilda?"

Virgil folded his hands behind his head and looked toward the ceiling. "I don't know what to think at this point. I never expected Ester to go missing. I can't think of a soul who'd murder Hilda. She's never bothered anyone that I know of. And I damn sure never expected Warren Hayes to show his face in this town again."

Cora adjusted her pillow and said, "If you were to have asked me a month ago, I'd have said Gibbs City was a nice quiet little town that's a great place to raise a family. Lately, I'm not so sure."

"Ethan and I are doing our best to enforce the law. I can't think of what else to do. It saddens me that Arthur may be looking at the kind of pain Hilda's husband, Mitch Weaver, is going through. And how in the hell am I going to find a murderer?"

"I'm still worried about the mining accident. That situation hasn't been settled yet."

"You're right. I expect any day for Ruth to file charges against Arthur. And he's mean enough to cause a lot of trouble."

"And there is still poor Ida."

"We could stay awake all night talking about all this stuff." He rolled over and captured her mouth, sending waves of pleasure through her body. "I'd much rather do something else."

She smiled, "So would I."

CHAPTET EIGHTEEN

Virgil was up and out the door before Cora woke for work. Today Maggie was taking the boys to school and he had to get to the station. The snow had stopped and rays from the rising sun shined bright as a summer day as he stepped off the porch.

The first place he went was to the site where they'd found Ester's car last night. In the light of day, things almost appeared normal. Nothing around the outside of the car made him think there was a struggle of any sort.

Overnight the door had become difficult to open due to the freezing weather. Brushing off the snow, he pulled on the handle. Inside, there was nothing that hinted at foul play or that there had been a struggle of any sort.

Removing a camera from the seat of his cruiser, he photographed the car and the surrounding area. It was eerily quiet out there early in the morning. But instead of feeling peaceful, Virgil's instincts told him this wasn't right. Something was amiss.

The car sat in the dead center of the road, facing the creek. It was clean inside without a trace of blood, thank God. But, if anything happened Sunday after Ester left their house, the snow would have covered it completely. That included footprints around the car or tire tracks from another vehicle.

Standing next to the automobile, Virgil couldn't figure out what had happened. Ester had probably driven the car there, but she wouldn't leave her purse behind. According to Arthur there was thirty dollars still in her wallet. That eliminated robbery. But where were the keys to the ignition? Someone had to take them.

Looking around the isolated location, Virgil tried to think of a reason Ester would drive out there to such a remote place. Most people avoided the area.

From all appearances, it looked like she'd driven from his house or town. There wasn't much beyond the area but a few abandoned mines that were sealed up tightly. The ground wasn't stable enough to build on. Black Water Creek swelled from the spring rains and that was the reason the mines finally had to close.

He arrived at the office just as the judge got out of his car across the street. Seeing Virgil, he waved and headed in his direction. Virgil put on a pot of coffee, dreading the meeting and wishing it wasn't the first thing in the morning.

"Mornin' Virgil. You have any news yet?"

He turned around and looked at the judge standing just inside the door with his hat in his hand. "On what case?"

"Any of them."

"No, nothing yet. I'm hoping something breaks today."

"Keep me posted. People are riding my back."

He turned to leave, but Virgil stopped him. "Listen, Francis, I know Ann Martin filed charges against Cora, but I'd like to explain."

"There's no need," the judge said, rather chipper.

"No, I don't think you understand."

Judge Garner turned to him, put his fists on his hips and spread his legs in a powerful stance. "But I do. Mrs. Martin came in complaining that Cora had hit her." The judge lifted his chin. "I can't say I wasn't surprised. But, even a saint can be tempted."

Virgil had no idea what Francis was talking about. "We are discussing the incident in the hospital yesterday afternoon where Cora punched Ann Martin in the nose, aren't we?"

"Yes, and the minute the bailiff made me aware of the complaint, I investigated. Then I had a call placed to Mrs. Martin telling her to kindly stay away from Dr. Carter unless she wanted to go to jail."

"What did she say to that?"

"I have no idea, the bailiff made the call."

"So, Cora's not in trouble?"

"Nurse Mae Price told me she saw the two women talking in the visitor's lounge in the hospital. Just as she went to turn away, Mrs. Martin raised her hand to strike Cora and your wife hit first." He brushed his hands together. "Clear case of self-defense and a good right hook. You might remember that in the future."

The tightness in Virgil's chest left and he felt like he could breathe for the first time since Cora told him about the incident. "I'm glad to hear that. We've been worried all night."

"I do suggest you warn Cora to think before she does anything like that again."

"I have Francis and I'll remind her again today. She regrets the incident, but she was provoked and she loves Jack." He poured a cup of coffee and held it out to the judge.

The man thought for a few minutes before accepting the mug.

With his own cup in hand, Virgil leaned against Ethan's desk. "We found Ester's car last night."

"I heard about that. Were you able to make any sense out of why she'd be out there in the boonies?"

Virgil shook his head, and blew on his coffee. "Nothing."

"Could she have been meeting a man out there? That used to be a popular place with the young folks a few years ago."

"I thought of that, but don't you think a woman Ester's age would rent a hotel or something? She's a little old to be smooching it up with a man in the backseat of a car, especially in freezing weather."

"True, but you never know about people."

"Who would she meet? And that still doesn't account for her not coming home. As close as she is to her father, I can't imagine her being that irresponsible."

After putting down his empty mug, Francis reached for the doorknob. "Let me know what you find out."

"I will."

When Ethan came in the three inspectors were right behind him. They looked happy to be leaving. Virgil walked into the outer office and put his hands on his hips. "You finish your report?"

Ebby handed him a file folder. "Here it is and we think you'll like our findings. We found that Arthur Bridges wasn't at fault, that the beams that crumbled weren't rotten enough to cause a direct threat to the men."

Virgil took the paperwork and made sure everything was in order. "It's not my liking you need to worry about. While I feel Arthur took appropriate actions, his crew leader didn't and should be reprimanded and fired. I don't see that in your report."

Rydal pulled on his gloves. "That decision is up to Arthur Bridges." He pointed at the papers in Virgil's hand. "Those are our findings."

Virgil narrowed his eyes and slid Rydal a contemptuous glare. "They might upset a few people."

Ebby shrugged with the confidence of a man who had the final say in the matter. "That's not our problem."

The men left the office, got into their vehicle and sped away.

Ethan poured himself a cup of coffee. "Well, they sure hightailed it out of here."

"They don't want to deal with the trouble this report is going to cause. Ollie Ruth is going to have a fit. I'm sure he has it on his mind to sue Arthur for negligence." Virgil waved the folder with a heavy sigh. "This prevents that from happening."

"You and I saw those timbers. While I'm no engineer, those beams were too rotten to properly support that entrance and should've been replaced months ago."

"I know," Virgil looked out the window at the courthouse. "I don't think anyone's going to be happy with this report."

"Probably not."

"Still nothing from Carthage?" Virgil asked. He wondered why Francis hadn't said anything earlier. Maybe he didn't want to face the obvious. Sooner or later, Ida Butcher would have to face the law for murdering her husband.

"I wonder why they're dragging their feet.

"No telling."

"Did you check out Ester's car?"

"Yes, I got up at daybreak." Virgil yawned. Last night he and Cora had stayed up late and this morning it was going to take a pot of coffee to wake him up. "I barely slept last night."

"I drove by there on the way in and I didn't see anything unusual or that caught my attention."

"But we both know she didn't just disappear into thin air."

"At the same time, Virgil, we don't have anything that says she was kidnapped, murdered, or even taken forcefully from the car."

"True. We don't know anything at this point. Is it a coincidence that a woman was murdered on the banks of Black Water Creek and another went missing a mile from the area?" Virgil stroked his chin. "Another thing that has me baffled is there hasn't been a ransom note. Nobody has asked Arthur for money."

"That's right."

"I tell you, I thought about this case most of the night. What would the two of them be doing down there in bad weather and obviously alone."

"Our job is to find out what happened and bring whoever is responsible to justice. The family members deserve that much."

"I agree," Ethan said. "I just don't know where to start."

"First, I'm going to have Carl tow the car to The Pit Stop Garage where we can examine it better. I couldn't find the car keys. Then I'd like to walk from where Ester went missing to where Hilda's body was found without all that snow flying in our faces."

"Wouldn't hurt. You may not find anything, but we won't know until you check it out."

Virgil finger-combed his hair and walked toward the coffee pot. "I don't know what else to do. The fresh snowfall is going to make it hard as hell to find anything."

The phone rang and Ethan answered while Virgil read the inspectors' report more carefully. In a town like Gibbs City, owners of mines were rarely thought of in a good light. That wasn't the case with Arthur.

He'd actually saved the Lucky Lady from closing so men would have jobs. But, when there was a cave-in, the nature of those once grateful people changed. Men making the big money became the scapegoats. Arthur was a businessman, but he cared about his employees.

Ethan hung up and turned to him. "That was the sheriff's office in Carthage."

"They want Ida delivered today?"

"No, the bailiff claims the sheriff says the judge has decided that she can stay where she's at until the trial."

Virgil rubbed his chin. "They're sure singing a different tune. Weren't they just kicking up dust wanting her out of Parker County and away from the judge's protection?"

"They were sure acting like we were a bunch of pea brains that didn't have the sense to keep a prisoner secure."

"Hum, I wonder if the judge knows all this."

"Guy didn't say, but since it will surely ease his mind, maybe you'd better let him know."

Virgil looked across the street. "I wish I knew more about what the future holds for Ida. There's no ruling on where her trial will be held, now?"

"Evidently not. I don't understand all this law stuff where they can make decisions about what happens to a prisoner." Ethan slumped in his chair behind his desk. "Ida is from this town, the crime was committed in our jurisdiction, and we have our own court system."

"I think the judge in Carthage found out Ida was staying at the judge's home instead of in jail awaiting trial. Also, she's been formally charged with murder and now out on bail. That doesn't usually happen."

"What harm is that? She's not exactly John Dillinger"

Virgil took his coat down from the tree near the door. "I'll see if the judge has time to see me and I'll try to get to the bottom of this." Putting on his hat, he turned back to Ethan. "Call me if you hear anything from the ME." As he walked out the door, he snatched the report off his desk.

"Sure."

Stepping out into the chilly air, Virgil hunkered down into his coat, anxious for spring. He'd had enough of the snow, being closed in, and his feet always cold. Out of the office, he passed several people on the streets going about their business.

The Lucky Lady employed about fifty people, and with the mine closed those people were all waiting to go back to work. Christmas was right around the corner and no one wanted to be without a job during this time of year. The sooner the mine opened the better.

Carl drove by and stopped in the middle of the road to chat. "Find out anything, Virgil?"

He held up the file. "Got the report back from the inspectors and it's not looking good."

"They want the mine shut down?"

"No, they didn't find anything wrong. Just a freak accident."

Carl frowned and stared out the windshield, his arm resting on the steering wheel. "That's not what the families of those dead men want to hear. They'll think someone should be blamed."

"I know that as well as you do, but I can't change a thing." Virgil leaned down and rested his folded arms on the edge of the door. "I feel they want to wash their hands of the whole damn mess."

"Leave it to those bigwigs at the Department of Safety Engineers and the Mining Association. They're damn good at hiding the truth."

"In most cases, but you and I know that Arthur didn't put any pressure on them to rig this report. He's too worried about Ester to concern himself with this."

"I just came back from helping Buford hook up the car. We're pulling it into the station. I'll put it in the last bay so you can move around there easier."

Virgil straightened. "Did you find anything unusual?"

Carl leaned over to the passenger seat. "I found this glove not too far away. It was covered with snow and I can't tell you how long it's been there, but it looked out of place."

Virgil took the evidence in his hand. Once frozen it was now wet and limp. Did he hold a valuable place of information in his hand? "Looks like a man's working glove."

"Those are pretty cheap at the dime store and almost anyone who works for a living has several pair."

"I have a couple myself," Virgil said. "Still there's no more reason for this to be out there than Ester's car. I'll take it inside and hold on to it should we find the matching one."

Carl propped his elbow out the window. "Even if you do, you'd never be able to identify who they belong to. There are hundreds of pairs of them in this town alone."

"Well, it's something and right now we have nothing."

Carl put the car in gear. "I have to get back to work. Let me know if we can help."

Virgil turned and retraced his footsteps back to the office, when his hand touched the doorknob, he looked up and saw Arthur coming toward him and he looked even more worried than the night before.

CHAPTER NINETEEN

Cora woke up alone. She knew before lifting her head that Virgil had already left the house. He was probably gone as soon as the sun came up. He wanted to get back to Ester's car to see if there was anything there that would give him any idea of what had happened.

She washed and slipped into a shirtdress gathered at the waist. If all went well, she wouldn't be wearing tight fitting clothes much longer. Touching her tummy gently she smiled and sent up a silent prayer that all would go well.

Getting Jack off to school had been a huge task. He didn't want to get out of bed, didn't want to brush his teeth and wasn't hungry when he sat at the table.

Cora sat beside him and smoothed down his brown hair. "What's wrong, Jack?"

He propped his elbows on the table and rested his chin on the backs of his palms, a disgruntled look on his face. "I don't know."

"Do you not want to go to school?"

"I don't know."

"Well, you'll miss your classmates."

"I know, but I can't wait for Christmas."

"That isn't far away. Aren't the students putting on a play this year?"

Jack twisted his mouth, and sunk lower to the table. "I guess. But me and Tommy didn't get picked for nothing."

So, that was it. The biggest play of the year and Jack and Tommy had been left out. That didn't make any child happy, especially one as outgoing and friendly as her nephew. "No part at all?"

"Nope, we just get to paint the scenery and that's boring."

Cora poured a cup of coffee and put a warm bowl of oatmeal with raisins in front of the young boy, who ate automatically.

"You can make any job as exciting as you want. That's up to you."

"But, Miss Potter tells us what to paint and the colors it needs to be. Tommy and me are just worker bees."

"It takes everyone to run a hive." She took a sip of coffee and smiled. "You and Tommy need to find something fun about your contributions to the play. Make it special."

Turning, Jack looked at her, his brows low. "I don't think that will work. Miss Potter has it all figured out."

"Well, you and Tommy need to come up with an idea that will change all that."

Before Jack could say anything, Maggie came in the door. "Mornin', is Jack ready?"

"Yes, we just need to get his coat."

As he ran toward the front door, Cora looked at Maggie. "Is Tommy down in the dumps about not having a part in the Christmas play?"

Maggie scowled. "Oh yeah, he's claiming he's not going."

"Jack was kind of moody about it today also."

"I know Miss Potter can't have every kid in the class in the play, but there should be something every child in the class can participate in during the performance."

"Since the class is so small, you'd think she'd come up with something for each kid to do so they all feel special."

"I might talk to her," Maggie said. "I don't want Tommy's Christmas ruined."

"Good, let me know what you find out."

Cora arrived at the hospital, went to her office and slipped on her lab coat then went to the nurse's station. Picking up several charts, she asked. "Anything unusual happen last night?"

"One of the nurses who'd just come on duty handed her a file. "It appears Mr. Hayes gave the staff a horrible time last night."

Studying the scrawl on the chart, she closed it and handed it back to the nurse. "He's not my patient, but check with Dr. Adams and suggest a sleeping sedative. That should help."

From behind her, a man cleared his voice. Dread dripped off Cora's shoulders. Without looking she muttered, "Good Morning, Dr. Adams."

Not in the mood for another confrontation, she went to the first floor to visit an elderly patient that she feared would require being sent to the nursing home. Nothing Cora did seemed to help the patient.

As she walked out of the room, Dr. Adams waited in the corridor. "I'll advise you not to make suggestions about my patients."

"I was simply helping the nurses out. I'm not surprised he gave the staff a hard time. Mr. Hayes is a tyrant. He's an abusive bully and the nursing staff doesn't need that kind of treatment."

"He's still my responsibility and you need to keep your suggestions to yourself. I'm sick of you going around the hospital like you're the Chief of Staff. Well, you aren't. Dr. Janson is and if you keep interfering with my patients, I'll report you."

His round body vibrated with anger and saliva gathered in the corners of his mouth. The man was hopeless and so eaten up with jealousy he didn't know what to do.

"You can report me all you want. However, as a member of this staff I have the right and obligation to speak my mind. If you don't like it then I suggest you be a better doctor."

His face reddened and he clenched his fists. She took a step back when he tightened his jaw. Following her, he stood an inch from her face. "You will get yours, Dr. Carter. Don't you think for one minute you'll get away with insulting me."

Luckily for her, Dr. Lowery came around the corner. Adams had his back to the other doctor, but obviously Stan knew what was happening.

"Good morning, doctors" he called out, making Dr. Adams step back. With his normally generous smile, Stan rubbed his hands together. "It's freezing out there."

Dr. Adams didn't reply, he simply turned and walked away.

"What's up with him?" Stan asked, watching Dr. Adams retreat. "Not in a good mood today?"

"He's angry at me for suggesting after the difficult time the night nursing staff had with Mr. Hayes last night that they ask about sedating him."

"That seems reasonable."

"I don't think he'll ever be reasonable when it comes to me." She shook her head. "I'm getting a little concerned with his threats."

"He's been outright belligerent?"

"Yes, and if it continues, I'm going to file a complaint."

They walked to Stan's office.

"You should. I can speak with him, if you'd like."

She was getting uncomfortable around Adams and he was physically threatening her if not in words, by actions that were unacceptable. Waiting for her heart to return to normal, she took a chair in front of Dr. Lowery's desk and rubbed her forehead.

"I've dealt with this my whole career, but he seems so hostile and angry. I'm doing my job yet he's constantly finding reasons to undermine my actions."

"We don't need that. I'll talk to Janson."

Not wanting to be looked upon as a constant complainer, Cora stood to leave. She had to finish her rounds. "I don't think that Dr. Janson will take my side because he's as biased toward me as Dr. Adams. The both of them are trying to make it difficult for me to stay here."

"Then let's go to the board. Enough is enough. You deserve to work here and we're not going to tolerate insubordination from anyone."

Cora went about her duties but decided that soon she'd discuss this whole situation with Virgil. Right now he had too much on his mind to worry about her and a little work dispute, but Dr. Adams frightened her.

In her office, she called the school to make sure they didn't release Jack to anyone she hadn't authorized. While the school shouldn't have to protect Jack, Cora couldn't shake the fear that he'd be kidnapped and taken away from her.

Looking at her watch, she realized she'd missed lunch. Her stomach growled to confirm that information. She stood, rubbed the back of her neck and stood up. Reaching in her purse for some cash to buy her lunch, she jumped when Dr. Janson came into her office without knocking. He didn't look happy, and Cora's spine stiffened.

"Dr. Janson," she said as she prowled thorough her purse. "What can I do for you?"

"You can try getting along with other employees."

Her head shot up and she shoved her purse aside. "What employee are you talking about?"

"Dr. Adams." He shoved the chair in front of her desk aside and leaned closer. "Stan came to me today with your complaints. Just so you know, James has his own complaints."

She crossed her arms over her chest and stared him in the eyes. "I'm sure he does. Dr. Adam's biggest problem is he's insecure and I pose a threat to his competence as a doctor."

Dr. Janson glared at her with hate filled eyes. "How dare you say such a thing?"

Cora shrugged. She'd had this argument before. "It's true and nothing can change that. The question is, do you stand with a small, mean-spirited doctor like Adams, or do you solve the problem?"

"I run this hospital and no one talks to me like that."

"Then no one is being honest." She put her palms on her desk and leaned forward. "If this continues, I'm going to the

Board of Directors and putting a stop to Dr. Adams harassing and threatening me every time he sees me." "How is he threatening you?"

"He keeps saying, I'll get what's coming to me."

Dr. Janson turned slightly and reached for the door. "Maybe he's telling the truth."

Her heart in her throat, Cora slumped back in her chair and took a deep breath. Chills danced over her entire body. They were both out to get her and she had no way of defending her job or her life.

Nurse Price tapped on her door and asked if she was going to lunch. Cora was certainly glad to see a friendly face. "Yes, I'm starving."

Mae smiled all the way to her warm brown eyes. "You're eating for two now."

Cora and Mae moved toward the elevator. "I am finding that I want to eat more."

"That's normal. Especially if you had morning sickness early in the pregnancy. It's like your body wants to make up for all the meals you missed."

With the confrontation with Drs. Janson and Adams behind her, Cora chuckled. "That must be it then. Last night I wanted brownies so badly I ended up baking them at bedtime."

"I had a thing for strawberries when I carried my first. Thank God it was summertime."

They found a table and sat down with their trays. After opening her drink, Cora looked across the table. "Do you know much about Dr. Adams?"

"Only that none of the nurses like him, except Hill and she's the worst nurse in the building."

"He's awfully mean."

Mae took a bite of her sandwich and chewed slowly. After swallowing, she said, "Stay away from him if you can. He's known for getting rid of people he doesn't like."

"Is he married?"

Mae thought for a moment. "You know, I don't have a clue. In all the years I've worked here, not once have I heard a word about his personal life."

"That's strange since we all work so closely together. I'm sure the board has annual dinners where the spouses and doctors attend together."

Several nurses walked by and greeted them on their way back to work. The cafeteria was busy this time of day and most employees either brought their lunch and grabbed a drink or snack, or bought a complete lunch like she and Mae enjoyed. The noise of the dishes and people filled the air.

"He really has it out for me. Even to the point he's threatening me physically."

Mae's brows rose. "Then you'd better report him to Dr. Janson before something happens."

"Janson paid me a visit earlier." Cora popped a chip in her mouth and chewed. "He's on Adam's side of this situation."

"You can always go to the board."

"I don't want to stir up that much trouble. It might make it worse."

Mae reached over and touched her arm. "Cora, this could be serious. Dr. Adams is capable of anything."

That surprised her. Mae wasn't one to spread gossip or talk badly about anyone, so her guess was that Adams was as bad as she'd first assumed.

CHAPTER TWENTY

Virgil walked across the street to the courthouse. The judge was at his desk going over papers when he entered the room.

"I heard from Carthage," Virgil said as he took a chair. "They claim Ida is to stay in the county and this is where she'll be standing trial."

He wasn't sure if the judge knew that bit of information or not until he physically slumped in his chair, and released a pent-up breath.

"Thank God there are people there who have a brain in their head."

"I take it you didn't know that?" Virgil said.

"No, but I've pulled every string I have to make it happen." He looked out the window. "Ida doesn't belong behind bars."

Propping his ankle on his knee, Virgil said. "I agree. Now let's hope the residents of Gibbs City can come back with a not guilty verdict."

"I going to try to get the whole thing dismissed on grounds of cruelty and self-preservation."

Relaxing in the chair, Virgil shoved his jacket off his shoulders. "That won't be easy."

The judge looked at him with such determination, Virgil nearly scooted back his chair. "I don't care. I'll defend her with everything I've got."

"She clearly had a rough life with Butcher."

"And it was all my fault."

Virgil wondered about his friend's state of mind. Maybe all this had been too much for him. Perhaps he'd fallen in love with Ida and didn't want to lose her, or he could be just talking foolishness.

"I don't understand."

"Ida Butcher was engaged to my younger brother. He was completely moonstruck by her. Days before the wedding he and I went out ice skating, the ice broke and he drowned. I was to blame because I panicked and moved back to safety. I didn't even try to save my own brother."

"That doesn't make it your fault. You might've ended up dead yourself." Virgil leaned forward. "We all have a normal instinct to save ourselves. It's only natural."

The judge pinned him with a powerful stare. "You don't."

"What?"

"I've seen you run into fires, chase after armed men, crawl down dark alleys, even be hoisted down into a collapsed mine."

Uncomfortable beneath his friend's evaluation, Virgil cleared his throat and squirmed in his chair. "That's my job."

"No, you're brave."

Virgil came to his feet and stepped away from the desk. "Now don't go talking foolishness like that. I do what I can for the people under my protection."

"My brother was under mine."

"Francis, stop. You're doing the best you can to make things better for Ida, but you can't take the blame for your brother's death any more than I can for all the men I lost under me in the war."

"I bet you're still haunted by that."

Virgil would never admit how badly those losses disturbed his peace of mind. "I try not to be. A man can only do so much."

Francis shook his head and reached for his pipe. "Life is sometimes tragic."

"There's enough of that right here in our little corner of the world." He handed Francis the file containing the inspectors' report on the mine cave-in. "I don't know if you'll agree with this or not."

After studying it for several minutes, Francis looked at him. "What do you think?"

"Well, I'm glad they didn't crucify Arthur, but there is some blame in all this and they didn't mention a word of it."

"You're right."

"He had a responsibility to make sure Cap replaced those timbers when he first reported them."

"Have you checked to see if he did?"

"No, but that's my next stop."

"I think Winston should lose his job," Francis said. "Clearly he's not keeping his men safe."

"I feel the same way."

Looking over the top of the report, Francis said, "Ruth's not going to like this. I'm sure he's expecting to make some money off this mess."

"I think they all are. Freeman will be compensated for his broken leg. And Ruth and Watters no doubt want something for the death of their sons."

"It's going to cost Arthur no matter how it all turns out."

Virgil let out a breath. "I think Arthur will close down the mine and that leaves fifty men out of work right here at the holidays."

Francis flipped several pages of the report. "It says here that as soon as the timbers are repaired and the site cleared, the mine is stable and can open."

"That's what the report says, not Arthur. He's pretty upset."

Francis threw the report on his desk. "Not to mention Ester missing. You have anything on that?"

Virgil shook his head. "Not a damn thing. Ethan and I can't even piece together what happened."

"Foul play?"

"No doubt." Virgil sat, propped his elbows on the arms of the chair and pleated his fingers. "Ester would never stay away from her father and daughter this long. She's either dead or someone or something is keeping her from her family."

"You check out Ruth? God knows he's capable of anything."

"I'm going to later today. But, I can't go accusing him of anything without some kind of evidence."

"You can ask any man or woman in this town if they've seen a missing person."

"If Ruth knows anything, you think he'd admit it?"

"No."

Virgil stood and pulled on his coat. "I've got several things to do. The good news for you is that for now Ida is in your care."

"Did you say that Ida once mentioned to John that Ervin had been abusive?"

"Yes. She told me that the night she killed Ervin."

"Why didn't John do anything?"

"I can't say, Francis. I wish he had, but it's hard for me to arrest a man for mistreating his wife. Look how hard it was to do anything to Hayes for the way he treated an innocent child."

"Yes, that was rough." The judge looked at him. "How's he doing?"

"Still in the hospital, but as soon as he's well enough, he's off to jail for attempted murder. I'm not messing around with that fool anymore. His ass belongs behind bars and I'm putting him there."

"I won't oppose you."

"Nobody better. That man pointed a gun at my wife's head."

Virgil left, his next stop the dry cleaners. Entering the shop, he greeted Helen and Nell. They were both thrilled that Cora was expecting and carried on about a baby shower of some kind.

The minute Virgil stepped into Arthur's office, his friend's head came up and a hopeful look crossed his haggard face. Virgil stoically shook his head. "We haven't heard anything yet." He pulled out a chair and sat down. "I'll let you know the minute we do."

"Thank you, Virgil, I know you're doing the best you can."

"I don't suppose you've heard from her have you?"

"No, not a word. Now Alice is home and she's worried half-sick about her mother. I drove around town this morning. I hoped she might have tried to walk home. I saw nothing."

"No one has contacted you about a ransom have they?"

"Not yet, but I have to be honest, I'd give every dime I have to get her back."

"Let's hope it doesn't come to that. I realize this is difficult for you and your granddaughter."

Arthur ran his trembling fingers through his hair and slowly shook his head. "I just wish I knew something. If I knew she was..." Unable to finish his sentence, Arthur slumped back in his chair.

"We'll find out what's going on." Virgil placed the report on Arthur's desk. "Here's the inspector's report."

Wearily Arthur stared at the folder but didn't touch it. "That's another mess." He shook his head. "I wish I'd never bought that mine."

"Well, you can't turn back time."

"Are they filing charges?"

Virgil shook his head.

"Big fine?"

"None of that. They basically reported that it was just an unforeseeable accident."

Arthur leaned back in his chair and gave Virgil a hard stare. "That's not right."

"That's between you and your employees at the mine."

Arthur finally picked up the paperwork and flipped through the pages. "People aren't going to like this one bit."

"They never do unless the owner is heavily fined, there are demands for improvements, and money flows into everyone's hands."

"I'd planned all along to take care of the people, Virgil. I know that the Watters' and Ruth's deserve something for the loss of their children. Believe me, with my own missing right now, I know how they feel."

"There was no doubt in my mind or anyone else's that you're a fair and just man."

"Those damned engineers don't know what the hell they're doing. Do you feel the mine is safe, Virgil? Would you go down there and do a thorough investigation so I can put those men back to work with confidence?"

"I'm no expert. You'd be better off to ask old Sandy Brown."

Virgil looked confused for a moment then said, "Do you mean the old guy that goes by, Whitey?"

Virgil nodded. "He's been in every mine around here since he was twelve years old. Nobody's better than he is at knowing these places. I trust him a helluva lot more than some engineer."

"I'll do that, Virgil. He's retired, but he knows the business all right."

"You might consider having him run the Lucky Lady for you. He's good, careful and he knows how to take care of the men while they're underground. The miners trust him, too. That's important."

"I hadn't given him a second thought, but he's perfect for the job. Think he'll take it?"

Virgil shrugged. "Don't know until you ask." Coming to his feet, he picked up the folder. "I have to file this in the courthouse. I just wanted you to see it first."

"I appreciate that."

Virgil was reluctant, but as he turned toward the door, he asked, "When was the first time Cap came to you about replacing the timbers in that section of the mine?"

"I think it was a month or two. I gave him instructions to immediately get the lumber, stop production and make the proper repairs. I even told Dabney Smith to make sure the lumber was ordered. When I asked Cap, he said the job was done."

"If I were you, I'd fire Cap. He didn't do his job and it cost lives."

"And he lied on top of that."

"Not a man you want or need."

"I'll take care of it.

CHAPTER TWENTY-ONE

Cora's day had been horrendous and then her name was announced over the PA system to report to the emergency room. Several patients had arrived due to a car wreck and her assistance was needed.

After two hours, she headed back to her office when a wave of dizziness washed over her as she stepped out of the elevator. She moved over for the wall to help support her should her legs buckle.

"You okay, Dr. Carter?" Mae asked. She took her by the arms. "Let's step in here and you sit down."

Mae led her to an empty patient's room and Cora found a ladder backed chair in the corner and eased down. "I don't know what came over me."

"Probably nothing," Mae assured her. "Just a little woozy, that's all. It's normal."

As a doctor Cora knew that, but it simply hadn't registered. Rubbing her forehead she waited should the feeling return. After several minutes, she stood and found the light-headedness had left. "I think I'll be okay," she took Mae. "Thank you for your help."

"You might want to go to your office and rest for a few minutes." Mae looked around then leaned closer. "Stay off the elevator. I couldn't get on one the whole time I was pregnant with my last child."

"Good advice."

More embarrassed than anything else, Cora went to her office and closed the door. After pouring a glass of water, she sat behind her desk and closed her eyes.

Suddenly she was so tired she was tempted to go home for the rest of the day. But she stayed because everything was normal and she didn't want to use her pregnancy as an excuse.

She decided resting for a few minutes was a good idea. Folding her arms on her desk, she laid down her head and thought of how wonderful it would feel holding her baby to her breasts. The next thing she knew, Virgil was shaking her awake.

"You okay?"

She looked into his warm blue eyes marred by concern and blinked several times. "I'm fine. Just a little tired." She straightened and stretched out her arms with a wide yawn. "I think I might have fallen asleep."

"We haven't talked about it, but maybe it wouldn't be a bad idea for you to quit working."

She loved her work and the thought of not coming to the hospital depressed her. Yes, she knew once the baby came she'd probably feel differently, but for now this was what she looked forward to. "I want to continue where I'm at. I'd be bored sitting home waiting for the baby to be born."

"But, if you're tired."

"That's normal in the beginning. I'll get better." She smiled at him from across her desk. "Be thankful the nausea is gone. That was the worst."

Virgil sat down but the wary way he watched her said he wasn't convinced one bit and nothing she could say would change his mind. "Still, you get any worse and I want you home."

"Who's the doctor in this family? I'll discuss me being home if I actually get sick or there's a danger to the baby. Nothing else."

He wasn't happy with her answer, but she could tell by his slanted eyes that he was watching her and the argument wasn't over yet. "We need to tell Jack."

Leaning back, Virgil said. "You're right. I think the whole town knows but him."

"And I don't want him to learn he's going have a new cousin from someone else," Virgil said.

Suddenly the situation with Ann, Jack, Dan and Virgil filled her mind. "I want us to try to adopt Jack."

Virgil smiled broadly. "I'm for that. He's like my son anyway."

"You know there will be problems. Thanks to his other family the process won't be easy."

"Have you talked to JJ? He's usually the one you turn to for legal advice."

She smiled. "While you go right to the judge."

Virgil's smile slipped. "Francis has enough on his plate right now."

"Have they come for Ida?"

"No, and the sheriff there claims they won't be taking her to Carthage to stand trial."

That was a surprise. "What changed their minds?"

Virgil shook his head. "No rhyme or reason for that to happen unless the judge extended his power far enough to reach the higher ups."

"I'm glad. At least she'll stand a better chance here."

"I learned today that the judge is going to try to get the charges dismissed completely."

Surprised, Cora stared at Virgil. "Can he do that?"

"I don't know, but he's going to damn well try."

Cora reached out her hand and he wrapped his fingers around hers. "I hope he can do that. No man has the right to hurt his wife."

"I agree and nothing makes me madder. Women can't defend themselves against a man. Poor little Ida didn't stand a chance in hell. Ervin was three times her size."

"I hate to think what would've happened to her young girls. Their future wasn't looking good."

"Well, let's hope things work out the way we want them to."

"Yes, and tonight let's tell Jack about the baby."

"What about the adoption?"

"Let me talk to JJ first." She averted her gaze. "I still have that incident with Ann to clear up."

"No, that's not an issue anymore. It appears Mae Price saw Ann raise her hand to you first."

Cora thought back. She didn't think anyone else was in the area. Was Mae lying for her? But, she told the absolute truth. "How did you find that out? Did you ask Mae?"

"No, it appears Mae saw Ann going into the courthouse and she surmised her intention was to lodge a complaint about you. So, she called the judge before Ann even got in the door."

"How strange." Funny that little went on in their small town without someone seeing something, yet no one knew a thing about Ester's disappearance. "She just saw her out of the blue."

Virgil squeezed her hand and grinned. "You forget, she lives at the fire station. The courthouse is right across the street."

That was true, it could've happened like Virgil said, or the judge could be a little prejudiced in her favor. Either way, it was the truth. Cora didn't think she'd have struck Ann if she hadn't raised her hand first.

Besides, Ann had no business coming to Gibbs City and trying to take Jack out of school. What if she'd actually gotten away with it? How on earth would they have gotten him back?

"I guess around here most things work out."

"That's kind of the way life goes."

"Have you heard from the Medical Examiner yet?"

"No, that's actually one of the reasons I'm here. Hopefully they'll know something because this case is a complete puzzle."

"Any word from Ester yet?"

"Not a single thing and this is the third day. Ethan talked to her friend, but came up empty handed. With each passing day I fear our chances of finding her alive grow slimmer and slimmer."

Cora brushed her palms over her face. How horrible for Arthur. Her concern went out to the elderly man. He was a kind man and had always been very nice to her and the people who worked for him. Now, he had to deal with this tragedy. "How's Arthur holding up?"

"The engineers gave me their report on the mining accident and that went in his favor."

"Oh," she said, leaning back. "How?"

"They claimed it was just an accident. No one was to blame."

"What does that mean, exactly?"

"It means that no one can sue or hold Arthur responsible for the mishap. I know that as the owner of the mine he'll do the right thing, but it might not be enough according to those involved."

"Meaning they may want more money than Arthur's willing to pay?"

"Exactly, I know Ollie Ruth would like to get every dime he has. Probably the same holds true for Lyle Watters."

"That was a terrible accident. Do you agree with their findings?"

"No I don't. Winston, who goes by Cap, should've made repairs weeks, if not months ago, but he didn't. While Arthur doesn't go down in the mine, it's not always wise to assume those telling you things are done are truthful."

"You're right, but a man Arthur's age shouldn't be going down into a mine."

"I don't know but this has sure put a damper on our Christmas holiday."

"I saw the big tree in the town square. When will it be decorated?"

"Usually it's all lit up by now. Arthur is the one who leads that whole thing. He has the decorations, and usually gets the school children involved and we have a tree lighting ceremony. It's a big celebration. But not this year."

"Maybe we can do something else. It's like this whole town is under a dark shadow."

"It is. With Hilda murdered, the mine cave-in and Ester missing, it's hard to think about celebrating."

"But the children don't know that."

"We should do it at least for them," Virgil said.

"I agree." She pointed at him. "Jack is anxious to go cut down a tree. You've been promising him for a week."

"We'll do it tonight?"

"Don't you dare wait until it's dark. Being in the woods during that time might scare him. Remember this is a brand new experience for him. That reminds me, I need to get some decorations."

"We'll do it right after school." He stood, walked around her desk and leaned down and kissed her gently on the mouth. He tasted delicious and his touch filled her with love. "I'm going downstairs to check with the ME. I'll see you at home tonight."

She called out. "With a Christmas tree."

As he left she smiled. Things weren't perfect right now, but children didn't know that and she wanted this to be a Christmas Jack would remember.

CHAPTER TWENTY-TWO

Virgil didn't make it to the end of the hall before Ollie Ruth came up to him and poked him in the chest. "So, you and Arthur rigged the report so me and my family couldn't get anything for our son being murdered in that damn stinking mine."

Virgil stared down at the chubby man who'd lost most of his teeth and hair. "Don't you ever lay a hand on me again or I'll slap my cuffs on you and haul your ass to jail. Neither Arthur nor I had anything to do with that report."

Back against the wall, Ruth shook his fist. "That's a lie. You're all liars. Cheating me out of what's rightfully mine."

"Arthur plans to do right by you, Ruth. But right now he's concerned about his only child."

His round face twisted into an ugly snarl. "He's getting what he deserves. Acting all highfalutin' with his fancy car and that castle he lives in. He deserves to suffer like the rest of us."

Virgil stepped closer, his heart thudding loudly. "What are you saying, Ruth? Did you have something to do with Ester's disappearance?" Virgil grabbed him by the lapels of his coat and shook the man. "Did you hurt her?"

Ruth struggled until he broke Virgil's grip. "I ain't done nothing and you can't prove I have."

Virgil pointed his finger and tightened his jaw. "If I find out you harmed that woman you'll go to prison and never see the light of day."

"I told you, I ain't done nothing, but that old coot is getting exactly what he deserves." Ruth straightened his coat. "I'm getting me a lawyer." He stomped out of the hospital, leaving his hat discarded on the floor.

Cora ran up to him. "What's happening? I heard shouting?"

"It was just Ruth being unreasonable." Watching the man shove through the door, Virgil wondered if Ruth had taken matters into his own hands. If so, Ester could easily be dead.

Cora grasped his arm. "You be careful. If he'd hurt one person, he'd hurt another."

Putting on his hat, Virgil made his way downstairs to the morgue. He couldn't get the thought out of his mind that Ruth would do something like kidnap or even murder Ester to spite Arthur.

Did she disappear as a result of the mine cave-in? Was she taken to make a point, to punish Arthur? He found that hard to believe, but when he got back to the office he planned to investigate further. Grief could make people do the unthinkable.

In the morgue, Virgil found the Medical Examiner sitting on a stool, bent over looking into the lens of a microscope. "Excuse me, I came to see if you'd found out anything on the Weaver body yet?"

Dr. Hutchins raised his head, and moved his glasses from his forehead to rest on his nose. Looking out through the thick lens, the stout man with a thin mustache looked confused for a moment. "What body?"

"Hilda Weaver?"

He held up his hand and motioned for Virgil to follow him. They entered a chilly room that was surrounded by silver lockers with pull handles. Usually several were kept for those who'd died of natural causes, but couldn't be buried until the ground thawed, others there were recently deceased.

Hilda Weaver was the only murder victim in the room and he suspected it was her body hidden beneath the white sheet on the table in the middle of the room.

"I finished the examination earlier this morning." He looked at Virgil. "I intended to call before leaving today."

"Much obliged." Virgil moved closer.

Dr. Hutchins reached over and folded back the sheet exposing Hilda's, pale, lifeless head. "This is the wound that caused her death."

Virgil looked down at a jagged wound on the lower left side of her head. Strange how he'd seen much larger injuries after a battle and the soldiers walked away. No one could ever tell about a head wound.

"What was she hit with?"

"I don't know. A blunt object because there are no smooth edges."

Virgil hated that such a young pretty woman would end up on a gurney in the morgue. Mitch Weaver had to be half out of his mind with grief. "Could she have been knocked down and her head maybe hit a rock?"

"There are no other wounds on her body. If she'd fallen her hands would've been scratched." He held up the lifeless palm. "Clean."

"Everything else normal?"

"She was pregnant."

Mitch hasn't said anything about that. "How far along?"

"Less than two months. I doubt she even knew for certain she was with child."

"You found no signs that she fought with someone, ran for her life, or any other physical damage?"

"No, there was nothing."

"So, someone came up behind her and smashed her in the head and caught her before she hit the ground."

"I don't know if that's how it happened. She might've known her attacker, or she was caught by surprise. When she was struck, she was looking away from the killer."

"Okay, we'll continue to search for anything that might point to who did this."

"I'm finishing up the paperwork. Her husband came by and I showed him the body. He wanted to know when it would be released for burial. I told him the undertaker could have the body tomorrow, unless you object."

Virgil shook his head. "No, that's fine." He turned to leave then decided on a few more questions. "How did Mr. Weaver appear when he saw his wife?"

Dr. Hutchins looked around the room, as if the words he needed were written on the walls. "Remorseful, tired, and sad. Very, very sad."

"Did you tell him about the child?"

"I did and if his brother hadn't had a good grip on him, he would've hit the floor. He wasn't aware he was going to be a father."

"How'd the brother appear?"

"Very supportive of his brother."

"You didn't find any old injuries, did you?"

Dr. Hutchins adjusted his glasses. "Excuse me?"

"Any sign she'd been abused in the past."

Dr. Hutchins firmly shook his head. "No, absolutely not. There was a small fracture on her collarbone that had healed, but I assume that either happened at birth or when she was very young."

Before leaving the hospital, Virgil stopped briefly to see how Roger Freeman was doing. His broken leg was getting better and he'd be going home in the morning.

Inside his office, he found Ethan talking to Lyle Watters. Virgil removed his hat and coat and hung them up. "What's going on here?"

Lyle looked as worn out as a bald tire. He hadn't shaved in a few days and grief soured his expression. "I wanted to find out if it's true about Arthur getting off scot-free."

"Believe me, he's suffering."

"Not like us, he ain't."

"He's got the mine to worry about and his missing daughter."

"Maybe she's dead."

Virgil stepped closer. "We sure hope that isn't the case. If it is, someone will end up in jail for life or executed."

Lyle shrugged. "If they get caught."

Sliding Lyle a determined glance, Virgil said, "I'll catch them. Don't you worry."

Heading for the door, Lyle said, "I'm not worried. I'm just saying sometimes there ain't no body to find."

"She'll be found."

Lyle left the office and Virgil and Ethan shared a surprised look.

"I swear between him, Ruth and anyone else working for the mine, I don't know what to think."

Ethan shrugged. "Lyle is just grieving over the loss of his son. If I was to point a finger at anyone it'd be Ruth. He's a damn troublemaker to begin with."

Virgil slumped in the chair and let out a breath. "I don't know who to trust. According to the Medical Examiner someone came up behind Hilda and hit her over the head with something."

"Really?"

"Yes, and she was expecting."

"Did Weaver know that?"

"No, he was pretty surprised when the ME told him."

"We don't have a single lead on Ester, either. I was hoping someone would come in with something. Surely people had to see her. She didn't just disappear."

Virgil looked at the clock on the wall. "I'm picking Jack up from school. After I drop off Tommy we're going to go chop down a Christmas tree."

Ethan looked out at the empty tree standing in the town square. "We really should decorate that. My kids keep wondering when they get to string the popcorn."

"I know. Cora and I were talking about that earlier. With so much going on, it's hard to celebrate even the birth of Christ."

"We have a tree up at home, but it's small. There isn't much to pick from this year."

"Really? I was thinking of checking on Highland Ridge."

Ethan shook his head. "Don't bother going there. Wasn't a thing over two feet."

"Hum, well I might look around then. Where'd you get yours?"

"Back behind Carolyn Williams' place. Her daddy planted a bunch of trees way back when I was a kid."

"I think Jack will just like the idea of cutting down a Christmas tree. According to Cora he's never done that before."

"Have fun."

At school, Tommy and Jack were the first two out the door. As they ran through the snow toward his car, he grinned. Those boys had more energy than they knew what do with. "Afternoon boys. How was school?"

"Boring," they said in unison.

From the top of the stairs, Miss Potter waved as they drove away. When they arrived home, Virgil took Tommy home and when Jack groaned in disappointment, he told him the plan.

Filled with excitement, Jack ran into the house to change out of his school clothes as Virgil went to the shed and found his ax. Fingering the blade, he quickly sharpened it, and locked the door behind him.

"Where you off to with that ax?" Earl called out. "You gonna chop off someone's head?"

Jack laughed. "We're going Christmas tree hunting. We're going to bring back the tallest one we can find."

Virgil ruffled his hair. "Whoa, remember we have to get it through the front door."

"Oh yeah." He turned back to Earl. "We're going to chop down the biggest one that fits in the house."

"That's more like it," Earl said. "Be careful out there that you don't hack off your arm."

Virgil wondered how stupid Earl thought him. "I know my way around an ax."

"Where you going looking?"

"I had thought of Highland Ridge but Ethan said there wasn't much there." Virgil slung the ax over his shoulder. "I haven't done this since I was a kid myself."

"Hate to mention it, but there are some nice looking furs over near Black Water Creek. From where I was standing they looked mighty good. But they're further up, near the north end."

"I'll check around." He took Jack's hand. "We'd better go before it gets dark."

CHAPTER TWENTY-THREE

Cora finished up work then accepted a lift from Stan. She knew Virgil and Jack were still probably out looking for a Christmas tree. She glanced over at Stan. "You have holiday plans?"

"I always go skiing. That's been my tradition for years."

"No tree, decorations or presents?"

"That's not for me. A friend and I always go to Colorado and spend the time in a nice warm cabin then we hit the slopes."

"Sounds like fun. I've skied once and that was all it took to convince me that wasn't for me."

They laughed.

"You know," Stan said. "You should get together with Nurse Price and set up a little party for the hospital. The place is like a dungeon."

"That would be fun and the patients would probably really enjoy it."

"Of course they would. A little holiday cheer goes a long way."

While they were alone, Cora debated discussing Dr. Adams with him but decided that should be done during working hours or she'd just be gossiping and she didn't want Stan to think that of her. "According to Virgil we're going to do the whole tree decorating, presents, and big dinner . His parents are coming to our house that day because I think Jack should be home on Christmas."

"I agree. I can remember every Christmas from the time I was three," Stan said. "My family always made it a huge event with relatives coming from all over. We'd spend half the day unwrapping presents."

She almost laughed at the irony because there were no fond memories for her at Christmas time. The only bright spot in her childhood was her sister Eleanor, and the Martin family had managed to take even that away from her.

Now she had Jack. When she took him she'd inwardly promised that his life would be different and it was. He would live in a house full of love and happiness.

"My childhood wasn't quite like that, but I do remember that St. Louis was lit up like nothing you'd ever seen before."

Stan glanced at her. "Gibbs City is a little more subtle, if you know what I mean."

"I'm sure it is."

"We'll probably be decorating the tree soon and the stores will be getting in the festive mood. Right now, with men laid off from the mine, I think the merchants are waiting to see how things go."

Cora cleared her throat. "Virgil said the report came back."

"That's good. I'm not a proponent for the mines, but they do provide jobs and men need those to take care of their families."

"It's too bad." She let out a deep breath.

They arrived at her house and she invited him in for coffee, but he had dinner plans that evening. Cora went inside and was immediately greeted by a tail wagging, barking, Pal. Reaching down, she scratched behind his ears and gave him a big hug. She removed her coat and hugged her arms. It was cold. Shivering, she adjusted the furnace a little and then stood on top of the vent until she thawed a little.

As she moved toward the kitchen, her phone rang. Not expecting Virgil and Jack to be home, she hoped it wasn't an emergency, although Virgil had a radio in his car.

"Hello."

"Good afternoon," Ann Martin's voice carried through the phone.

Her heart pounding, Cora asked, "What do you want?"

"I'm calling to tell you that I've hired a lawyer to help Dan get custody of his son."

"That doesn't scare me. The Martin name doesn't mean what it used to, Ann. You might very well regret a move like that. I know you were as much involved with your husband's crime syndicate as your son." She took a deep breath to steady her nerves. "If you pursue this I'm hiring a private investigator to look into Judge Martin's affairs more carefully. Also, Detective Batcher hasn't let up a bit. He's not going to quit until your whole family is behind bars."

"I'm aware that cop is shadowing me and my son. He needs to be careful nothing happens to him or his family."

"Really? If that happened you'd have Virgil to deal with and believe me you don't want that."

Having heard all she could stand, Cora slammed down the phone and went into the kitchen. She'd barely put the coffee on before Earl came through the door, his wiry gray hair sticking up, the pant legs to his overall stuffed in the tops of his boots, a wide grin on his face.

"Jack sure was excited about getting a tree."

She smiled. "I knew he would be. Too bad Virgil had to put it off so long."

"Aw, kids don't care. Once it's up and decorated, he'll be happy."

"I don't have one single ornament. I'll have to go to town this weekend and buy some."

Earl's head came up. "Don't do that. I have two big boxes full. Me and Wanda used to decorate a tree every year."

"But those are your memories."

"I haven't taken them out since Wanda passed. They're just taking up space."

"Well, if you don't mind, I'm sure Jack would be delighted to put them on the tree. They'd mean a lot more to me than new ones."

"I'll be glad to get rid of them. Like I said, I ain't got no use for them. My chopping down Christmas tree days are over."

She took two cups out of the cupboard. "Good. You can spend that day here with us. Virgil's family is coming over."

"How are Roy and Minnie? I hardly see them anymore."

"They're fine, but the Pit Stop keeps them pretty busy."

"In my opinion, Roy should've never closed down that filling station to begin with."

"I think he regrets it now."

"Carl and Buford are doing a good job of running the place. Stopped by there the other day and there was a line of cars waiting to get gas."

"That's wonderful. I'm glad Nell's husband was able to go into business with Carl. They're good people"

She took a chicken out of the icebox, put it under cool water then salted it before putting it in the oven to cook for dinner. Adding potatoes and carrots, she set off the flame and turned to make dinner rolls.

"How is work?" Earl asked. "You liking it there?"

"I love it except for Dr. Adams. He's so obnoxious to the entire staff. Lately, he's taken a special interest in annoying and threatening me."

Earl poured coffee. On the way back to the stove, he stopped. "What do you mean he's threatening you?"

She dusted her hands with flour. "Oh, you know how some people are about women doctors. He's so narrow minded I want to kick him in the pants."

"How exactly is he threatening you?"

"He goes on about how I'm going to get mine, and one more wrong move from me and I'll pay. I tell you the guy's an idiot."

Earl became too quiet to suit her.

She spun around, and said, "Now, don't you dare take that the wrong way. If he ever really stepped out of line, I'd tell Virgil right away."

"I don't know," Earl said. "With Ester missing I don't trust anyone."

"Well, Dr. Adams is all wind. Nothing you need to give a second thought to."

"In your condition, I don't want anyone threatening or making you mad. That doctor needs to find his manners or I'll go down there and give him a refresher course."

She smiled to herself. He was so protective of her and Jack. But, she had to admit that Dr. Adams was beginning to make her uncomfortable and she couldn't go to Dr. Janson to discuss the matter. Another incident and she'd say something to Virgil or better yet, she should take the matter to the board.

With supper cooking, Cora sat down to her warm cup of coffee. "Virgil said the engineers finished some kind of report about the cave-in at the mine."

"Did he say what they said?"

"Something about not blaming Arthur, which I'm glad. I know he feels horrible, and I've no doubt he'll be fair to those involved."

"Arthur is a good man. I've known him so long I can't remember the first time we met. The cave-in was a terrible thing but it tore him up. He really cares."

"I'm sure he does. I loved working for him and when he found out what Bart was up to, he put a stop to it immediately."

"That crazy Bart. I still can't believe what a cracked person he was. And when I heard that he'd tried to kill all of you in the Judge's chambers, I thought he'd lost his mind."

"Oh." She shivered. "Don't bring him up. That's a conversation I don't want to get into." She covered her ears. "I can still hear the sound of gunshots."

"I'm thankful he didn't hurt anyone. Good thinking on Carl's part."

She smiled. "I was so proud of him when he received his medal. He looked like a completely different man than I'd met months earlier."

"He sure turned a corner all right."

CHAPTER TWENTY-FOUR

Virgil and Jack weren't having much luck finding the right tree. There were several to choose from, but most were either too big or two small. They'd checked several places but had no luck.

Determined to get the perfect tree for their first Christmas, Virgil trudged toward the Black Water Creek area as Earl had indicated. It was pretty isolated, but from a distance he saw several possibilities. They had climbed the steep incline with Jack sliding back down twice.

The young boy was having a wonderful time, but he struggled to stay on his feet. They'd enjoyed the afternoon together in the outdoors on the hunt for a special tree that would decorate their home for the holidays. Virgil loved times like this when he and Jack were alone and could do what Jack affectionately called *man time."*

Watching him grow, Virgil was so proud he was in his life. Jack was a well-mannered young boy who, for the most part, stayed out of trouble and did well in school. He hadn't had friends before coming to Gibbs City. Hell, he hadn't had much of anything, but somehow he'd risen above all that and he and Tommy had created quite a bond.

He pointed up ahead. "Look Jack, we might have hit the jackpot."

"Yeah, I saw those. And they don't look too tall for the living room. Aunt Cora will be so surprised." Jack jumped up and down clapping his hands.

"Only if it's the right size and we don't have to hack it up to get it inside the house."

"No, we want it to be perfect to start with."

Jack trudged behind Virgil who steered them clear of the water. "The one Miss Potter put up in the classroom is too small and it's really skinny. And no matter how many decorations we put on it, the poor thing still looks kinda puny."

"Maybe she couldn't get anything better."

Jack caught up with him. "Well, we're going to get it just right." He looked up with a toothless grin. "I want Aunt Cora to be happy. Don't you?"

"I sure do. I don't think she had a lot of happy times growing up." Virgil remembered the trial and how it broke his heart to listen to her mother admitting she'd deliberately led Cora's father into believing she wasn't his child. What kind of person does that? A sick, disturbed one who now tried to get her daughter's sympathy.

Virgil had his eye on one particular tree that stood on the other side of the creek. From where they stood it looked the right height and the branches were full, making the tree perfectly round. He imagined it in the living room and grinned. This could be perfect.

He knelt down and pointed to the tree in question. "What about that one? It looks really good."

Jack followed his direction and his eyes widened along with his mouth. "That's a good one. Let's go get it."

As the boy took off, Virgil grabbed him by his collar and pulled him to a stop. "We can't get to it without going across the bridge. Let's get back in the car and we'll drive about a mile to cross over."

Jack looked at him. "I didn't know there was a bridge. I bet Tommy don't either."

"Probably not. There isn't much on the other side of the county line, but the only way to cross is farther down."

At the car, Jack crawled inside and closed the door. The heater kicked on, but little heat came out from under the dash. Virgil smiled at the way Jack's eyes followed the chosen tree until they reached the bridge. He had no idea when the thing had been built but it showed serious signs of age. Narrow, wooden and covered in snow, Virgil debated driving across.

He feared too much weight and the thing would crumble into the creek below and with the cold temps, if the fall didn't kill them, the freezing water would. "Looks like we better walk across. You okay with that?"

Eager to reach the prize, Jack grinned. "Sure."

Virgil grabbed the ax from the backseat and they headed toward the other side. "Be careful and stay close, Jack."

"I will."

Instead he ran ahead to stop in the middle then moved to the railing and looked down at the water from the view on the bridge. He put his booted feet on a ledge and gripped the rail. "It's not that far down."

"It's far enough if you were to fall."

They reached the other side and headed for the tree over the next rise. Virgil looked up and hoped it didn't start snowing. While he knew the area well, it was easy to get disoriented when you're surrounded by white stuff.

Off to the side, something captured his attention. Virgil stopped and looked into the distance. Jack ran toward the tree, grabbed the trunk and shook it like he'd seen him do earlier.

Virgil turned and walked in the opposite direction. "Where are you going?" Jack called out.

"Stay with me, son." As they drew closer, a rundown cabin came into view. Virgil stopped.

"Who lives there?"

Virgil had forgotten about that place. "I don't think anyone does. That place has been vacant for a long time. A man lived here once before the flood. We called him Hermit."

"Did Hermit move away?"

"No, that wasn't his name. We called him that because he wanted to be left alone. Never came into town or socialized with the rest of the townsfolk. He passed away when I was a teenager."

Virgil walked closer. Something about the place looked more recently used than it normally would after all these years of being vacant. The shack should've collapsed a long time ago. That told him that someone had gone to the trouble of keeping it upright.

After stopping, Virgil took Jack's hand and looked behind them. The place where Ester's car was found was only about a mile away. Hilda's body had been found further down toward town on the other side of the creek.

As his eyes scanned the snow-covered ground, nothing showed that there had been anyone in the area in a long time. However, it'd snowed heavily the day before and that would cover any tracks.

Jack pulled on his hand. "Uncle Virgil, are we going to chop down the tree?"

"In a minute." He released Jack and turned to him. "Stand right here. Don't move. I'm going to check out the cabin."

Jack looked around. "Can't I go with you?"

"Just a little closer. If there's anything in that cabin, I don't want you hurt."

The young boy stared at the shack and pointed at their prize. "Let's just get the tree and leave."

"We will. Wait for me."

Virgil approached slowly, carefully looking around. As he drew closer, he glanced back at Jack who stood in the clearing. He was frightened and Virgil wished he hadn't brought the boy up there. Three feet from the door, Virgil took his gun from the holster and stepped under the overhang.

If the solid wood door had been opened recently, the last snow covered up any evidence of activity. Frost covered the windows, making it impossible for him to see into the darkened, one room shack.

A sickening feeling settled in his stomach as he reached for the doorknob and turned gently. He moved forward but was stopped. Someone had locked the door.

Why secure the door? And who would bother?

His suspicion grew to an alarming point. Moving away from the door, Virgil tried to peer into the interior but couldn't make out a thing because the ice on the glass made it impossible. It was too obscure and dark.

"Come on, Uncle Virgil."

"Give me a minute, Jack." He looked back at the boy. "You stay right there."

Circling around, he heard nothing unusual and was about to join Jack so they could do what they came for, but just as he went to move away, he heard it again. The noise came from inside the cabin.

He didn't know what it was, and he couldn't identify anything. His gut instincts took over and Virgil went back to the door and kicked as hard as he could. The hinges creaked mournfully. Stepping back, he kicked again and the frame splintered. With one final boot slammed against the weakened wood, he'd crashed down the door.

Dust rose and tickled his nose, but when he sensed there wasn't a threat, he put his gun away and stepped inside. Only a table sat in the middle of the room. There were only pieces and remnants of articles of clothing, old, broken furniture and clutter.

In the corner, a heap of discarded clothing looked strange considering everything else was strewn around without any regard for where things belonged. He stepped close, and nudged the heap with the toe of his boot.

Nothing happened, but it was too solid to be clothing. Virgil turned, went to the door and called Jack closer. As the boy moved carefully, Virgil told him to stay on the porch where he could see him. Looking around, outside, Virgil didn't see anything.

Back to the clothing, Virgil leaned down and tossed items aside until he saw a hand and a coat sleeve. Quickly he moved aside all the debris and saw Ester lying on the floor tied to a chair, her head propped on a wad of dirty curtain.

"Jack," he called. "Get in here."

Eyes wide, Jack entered and stood beside him. "That's Mrs. Cooper." He leaned closer. "Is she dead?"

His finger on her pulse, he waited patiently. "Barely alive. Quick, we have to get her help."

Virgil picked up a half frozen Ester, and ran from the door. "Stay up with me, Jack. If we don't get her help soon she'll die."

Virgil heard Jack huffing and puffing to keep up. They reached the bridge and Jack darted ahead of him. "Open the back door, Jack."

Virgil took another step and the bridge beneath him gave out.

CHAPTER TWENTY-FIVE

After waiting over an hour, Cora and Earl sat down to eat dinner only to have Arthur knock on the door. Cora answered and invited him to join them. He reluctantly agreed but it took a lot of coaxing to get him to eat and then it was very little. She doubted he'd had a decent meal in days.

Earl pushed his plate aside. "I hear Virgil got the report today."

Arthur wiped his mouth then laid the napkin beside his plate. "Yes, I read it but I'm not sure I agree with it."

Cora put her folk down and reached for her coffee cup. "How so?"

"It's a full report. Almost five pages long, but it all comes down to it being an accident."

Earl rested his forearm on the table. "You don't agree."

Arthur's face reddened. "No, I don't. Winston told me he'd fixed those beams and the mine was safe and sound. Virgil said the wood was completely rotten."

"So old Cap lied," Earl said.

"He did and I don't know why."

Cora watched the two men. Their respect for each other was evident in the tone of their voices. No judgment, no harsh words and no one raised his voice. "You'd think your crew chief would want to save lives."

"Oh," Arthur said. "I'm sure he does, and he's upset about the cave-in, but it comes down to him not doing his job."

"That's not like Cap."

Cora rose and poured more coffee. "I've never met him. But I would imagine that safety is the most important thing in those mines."

"It is," Earl said. He looked at Arthur. "You plan to open the Lucky Lady?"

"I don't really want to, but those men need work. Especially this time of year." Arthur leaned his elbows on the table. "I had Whitey go down and check the place out earlier today. He said if that framework had been fixed, the mine wouldn't have caved."

Earl took a sip of his coffee, nodded then said, "He knows more about mining than anyone around here."

Arthur nodded. "That's what I figured. I talked to him about opening the mine. He thinks once the rubble is cleared and the roof reinforced, the area should be safe."

Earl looked at her. "I know a lot of people hate those mines and with good reason, but a lot of families depend on them."

"If you have them, at least make them as safe as possible," Cora said. "That's the least you owe those men."

"That's the only way it's going to be." Arthur turned his chair and propped his arm on the back. "I'm going to fire Winston tomorrow. Whitey has agreed to take over. I'll be speaking to all the miners so they know what's going on."

Earl smiled. "You always do what's best, Arthur. Everyone in this town admires you for that."

"Now I just want my daughter back."

Earl let out a loud breath. "I can't for the life of me figure that out." Earl averted his gaze. "I've always been of the mind that maybe Ruth did something foolish."

"I know that man hates my guts. He just left my house. Dropped by to tell me what he thought of me and how I paid off the inspector."

Earl snarled. "That dirty dog."

"He scared Alice to death. It took me hours to calm her down. That's why I'm here. I was wondering if Virgil can convince him to leave us alone."

"I don't blame you," Cora said. "How frightened she must've been."

"Virgil will set him straight."

"You know me, Earl. I intend to make it right by the families. I wouldn't do it any other way. I can't bring those boys back, but I owe the families."

"I know. Can't understand why Ruth can't get that through his thick head."

"He probably had great hopes of ruining you financially," Cora said. "I'm sure nothing would make him happier."

"If he did that, what about the other families I help?"

Earl swatted the air. "Aw, he don't care about nothing except what he wants. He's a mean, selfish bully. Always has been."

Arthur pushed back from the table and stood "You're right." He looked at Cora. "Thank you kindly for the meal. It was delicious. When Virgil returns, will you ask him to come see me tomorrow?"

Cora stood and took his hand. "Of course I will. I'm sure he and Jack will be home soon."

Arthur put on his coat and hat and left. Cora looked back at Earl. "I'm sorry your friend is suffering so much."

"I am, too, but Arthur's been through a lot. He'll be okay."

Cora brought the pot to the table. "I'm sure Virgil will find his daughter. Ester will be okay."

Earl stirred a spoon of sugar in his cup. "I don't know if I can believe that. She's been missing two days. If she's not somewhere safe, there's no way she can survive."

Cora looked out at the evening sky. It would be dark soon and Jack and Virgil weren't back. Where could they be? "Let's hope she's found soon."

"I thought the two boys would be back by now bragging about their great find."

"Me, too," she replied, wringing hands. "I hope nothing's wrong."

She heard the scrape of his chair then the touch of his hands on her shoulders. "Now, don't go worrying when you don't have to. Virgil knows his way around. They'll be here any minute."

Cora listened to her friend's words, but something wasn't right. It didn't take this long to cut down a tree and Virgil knew not to be in the woods after dark. Where could they be?

CHAPTER TWENTY-SIX

Virgil fell through a hole in the rotten planks, knocking Ester's body from his arms and sending her three feet away. She lay on the snowy bridge like a rag doll. Virgil hung from his forearms, the rest of his body hanging above the rapid water below. His elbows were the only things keeping him from falling.

He looked up. Jack had stopped and was heading back toward him. "Stop, Jack. Don't move."

The boy turned to stone. "I need to help you."

Virgil tried to pull himself up, but a jagged board stabbed into his back, keeping him in place. "Jack, listen to me," Virgil said. "It's important you do exactly as I say."

With his bottom lip trembling, Jack nodded.

"Do you know how to use the radio in my car?"

"No, but I seen you talk into it."

Struggling to hang on to his icy grip, Virgil said, "Go to the car..."

"No, I don't want to leave you."

Virgil knew time was critical. They needed immediate help. "You have to do what I say. No questions. You have to be brave or Ester and I are both going to die, Jack. This is serious."

Tears coursed down his cheeks and Virgil wished with all his heart he could take the young boy in his arms and reassure him that everything was going to be okay, but he couldn't. Not right now.

He repeated. "Go to the car. Take the radio off the hook and press the button on the right side of the mike. Hold it down while you talk. That's all there is to it."

"But, what do I say?"

"Tell Ethan we need help. We're at the Black Water Creek Bridge and I've fallen through a hole." Virgil looked at the lifeless body of Ester Cooper. "Tell him to send an ambulance, too."

"What if I can't do it?"

"Jack, you're a special little boy. You can do anything. Now go, because I can't hold on much longer."

Jack quickly turned and disappeared over the ledge as Virgil struggled to control the pain in his back. Wood worn weak by years of use groaned and Virgil closed his eyes. He prayed if the deck broke and he fell through, he'd survive if for no other reason than to get Jack home safely. He didn't want Jack to think he'd failed him.

Virgil waited for what seemed hours before the boy came up over the ledge. He stood at the edge of the bridge. "I think I got him. I couldn't hear him and it was all crackled."

The area was abandoned and the radio might not be in range. He hadn't thought of that. Gritting his teeth, Virgil pulled his body forward as hard as he could until the stick in his back came out.

He bit back a scream because he didn't want to scare Jack. He'd been through enough. Nearly weak from the effort, Virgil sucked in a deep breath and tried to pull up and out, but couldn't because of the slippery grip he had on the bridge.

It felt better without the dagger in his back, but he knew losing blood wasn't a good thing out here. "You okay, Jack?"

"Yeah, but I'm kind of scared."

"I am too, but we'll get out of this. No matter what happens don't think you didn't do everything you could to help me and Ester. You're a good boy and I love you."

"I love you to, Uncle Virgil. I don't want you to die."

Virgil shook his head. "I'm not going to die. I still have to chop down a Christmas tree."

"I don't care about an old tree," Jack cried. "I just want us to go home."

While one elbow supported his body weight, Virgil brushed away the snow and tried to clear a small patch where he could get a better grip. The snow went easily, but the ice beneath it remained. Placing his palm flat, Virgil pushed up just a little trying to gain more leverage.

He couldn't hang on forever and if help wasn't coming, he had to find a way out. He managed to wedge up a little only to quickly fall back down before he could lift his weight. Anxious to get off the bridge, Virgil held on with one arm and pounded on the wood beside him hoping to create a path to the edge where he could use the spokes in the railing to pull himself out.

However, the deck wouldn't budge. Virgil looked at Jack. "Can you make your way home from here?"

Jack looked around. "No, I've never been here and Tommy isn't with me."

"You can get home by going back toward town. Stay on the road. You'll come to the spot where you and Tommy found Hilda's body. You know how to get home from there."

"But it's almost dark."

"I know, but if you stay out here, you'll freeze Jack. You must run home as quickly as you can. It's your only hope."

"But what about you?"

He hated to lie, but he didn't have a choice. "Ethan is probably on the way to get me right now. You go ahead and do what I say. I want you home safe and warm with Aunt Cora. She's worried by now and she needs you."

Tears sprung anew. "We both need you. Uncle Virgil, I can't leave you."

"I'm not asking you, I'm telling you to go home."

"I can't."

"This is serious, Jack. You're shivering. You can't last and neither can I." Virgil gasped for a breath. "I can't stand the thought of anything happening to you."

Jack quickly disappeared and a wave of relief washed over Virgil. Hopefully, Jack would be safe and that was all that mattered. He looked at Ester and wished he'd been able to save her, but that wasn't meant to be.

"Uncle Virgil," he heard Jack call out. "Here's a rope." Before he could protest, Jack moved closer and tossed him the rope. Virgil grabbed it and almost lost his hold.

"Jack, we have a rope, but you aren't strong enough to tie a knot that will pull me out."

"I know that, Uncle Virgil but I slammed the other end in the trunk. Now hold on. I'm going to back up the car."

"Jack, Jack, stop."

The boy looked at him. "What?"

"You don't know how to drive. The front of the car is pointed toward the creek. If you don't get it into reverse, you'll go right into the water."

"Then I better get it right."

"Jack."

In a matter of seconds, the sound of the car engine filled the air and Virgil prepared to let go and get in the water in order to save Jack. Just as he raised one arm, a heavy tug pulled him forward. Not much, but enough for him to get his stomach onto the bridge and let the rope go.

Jumping to his feet, he ran toward the ledge to find Ethan behind the wheel with Jack on his lap. Virgil collapsed on the ground. He brushed aside tears of exhaustion. He'd been terrified Jack wouldn't know now to stop the car and end up killing himself.

By the time Ethan reached him, Virgil was weak with relief.

The emergency vehicle pulled up and together they got Ester into the ambulance. Ethan helped ease Virgil into the squad car. Gritting his teeth, he relaxed gently against the seat, his back on fire. Cora would be beside herself.

"When we get there, go pick up Cora. Don't tell her anything is wrong." He told Ethan.

"Oh yeah, like that's going to be easy."

He reached over and pulled Jack on his lap and into a giant hug. "You're the bravest and smartest little boy I know."

"I almost blew a gasket when I saw him trying to drive the squad car. I figured I'd better act quickly or I'd be fishing him out of the water."

"Then you did hear me, Uncle Ethan?"

"I heard Black Water Creek and knew I needed to check it out."

Virgil leaned his head against the headrest. "I'm glad you did."

"Did you see anything besides Ester?" Ethan asked. "I'll be there first thing tomorrow to check the place out."

"Not a single sign of life or any evidence that anyone had been there." Virgil rolled his head and looked at Ethan. "I didn't see a thing."

"What do you figure happened?"

"I think she was kidnapped, tied to that chair, fell over and managed somehow to get enough stuff on top of her to keep from freezing," Virgil said.

"I wonder if she tried to escape."

"The door was locked from both sides. She couldn't get out."

"Let's hope she makes it. I told the ambulance driver to call Mr. Bridges as soon as he gets to the hospital."

Virgil knew his back wasn't serious, but he might as well go because Cora would insist he have stitches if it was anything more than a scratch.

CHAPTER TWENTY-SEVEN

Cora nearly had a heart attack before Ethan finally pulled up at the hospital. She hadn't even bothered to button her coat. Instead, the minute he said Virgil and Jack were at the hospital she ran out of the house.

Ethan tried to reassure her on the way but she didn't hear half of what he said. While he had the sirens blaring and drove as fast as safely possible, she was still anxious. They stopped outside the hospital and she darted out of the car and through the double doors.

Inside the emergency room she slid back a long curtain and saw Virgil, his shirt removed and a blanket around his shoulders with Jack in his lap.

He looked up and gave her a crooked grin. "Hi," he said. "We're fine."

Cora's knees nearly buckled with relief. Although Ethan had reassured her, she couldn't believe Virgil was all right until she saw with her own eyes. "My God, what happened?"

"It's a long story, and I'd like to get home so Jack can get to bed. He has school tomorrow."

Stan entered the area and smiled. "Virgil is all stitched up..."

Cora's heart thudded loudly. "You had stitches? Where? Let me see."

"They're in his back and bandaged. He had a jagged board stab him and some splinters in his hands, but it's not serious, Cora. He's okay. He can go home."

She could have lost them both. For a minute Cora covered her face and said a quick prayer of thanks then she walked over and hugged Jack. "And what were you doing when all this happened, young man."

Jack shrugged nonchalantly. "Saving him."

Cora stepped back, looking down at her nephew. "What?"

"He pretty much did everything necessary to save my life. Even thinks he can drive a car."

Dear God, she couldn't believe her ears. Her hands shook and her mouth went dry. "You could've both been killed."

"I fell through the deck of a bridge and Jack found a rope, slammed one end in the trunk lid, and threw me the other."

Jack's face beamed, while Cora's knees shook. "Then I started the car so I could back up and pull Uncle Virgil free."

Cora grasped the edge of the gurney Virgil sat on and held on tightly. Her eyes moving from one to the other, she said, "That's so dangerous."

Jack thumbed to Virgil. "Course it was. I was saving his life. I watched Uncle Virgil drive so I knew what to do."

She took the boy by the arms. "You are never to put your life in danger. What if something would've happened to you? Uncle Virgil and I would be heartbroken."

Virgil pulled Jack closer against his side and frowned. "The boy saved my life. He's brave and courageous. Don't take that away from him."

Virgil stepped off the gurney and eased Jack down and helped him put on his coat. He smiled, and winked at the boy.

Ethan came in. "Your squad car is waiting outside." Ethan knelt down and shook Jack's hand. "You're a smart young man and you did a very brave thing today."

Virgil turned and slid his arm through the sleeves of his torn shirt and buttoned it close. Then he put on his own coat, and took Jack by the hand and walked out of the hospital.

"Thank God Jack saved your life. I didn't mean he wasn't brave," Cora said, trying to explain away her fear and her mother's instinct. "I don't want either of you hurt. You both mean the world to me."

Virgil turned to her. "Life doesn't come with any guarantees. If Jack hadn't somehow found the strength and cunning to help me out of that situation, I probably wouldn't be here." He walked purposely out of the building toward his car. "And no, I didn't ask him to help. I tried to send him home where he'd be safe."

Cora ran behind them. "He's just a child."

Virgil turned to her. "Jack is a very special boy. Under extreme pressure he used his head and did the most logical thing. Fear didn't stop him and neither did me telling him to go home. Don't take this lightly. I don't care how old he is."

He cupped her face and kissed her lips. "This young boy had no father to guide him, no love to nourish him and no promise of a successful outcome. He did what he did because he has heart. And that makes him special."

Tears flooded Cora's eyes as Virgil and Jack turned walked to the car. After he'd put her nephew in the backseat and closed the door he pulled her against him. "I know you're scared, sweetheart. That's only normal."

She said, "It is only normal that I would be frightened for both of you." She scowled at him. "You don't need to be making daring rescues either."

"I'll accept that. However, Jack is too smart for you to try to keep in a protected cage."

Her mouth opened but she knew it would take a while longer for her to get past her fear to speak. "I'm sorry. I never for one minute thought that Jack would not be up to the task, any task. I'm just afraid of losing him and if that's wrong, then I'm guilty and proud of it."

She walked around the car and got in on the other side. After closing the door, Virgil carefully placed himself behind the wheel and they left for home.

"Aunt Cora," Jack said softly. "I didn't have to drive the car. Uncle Ethan came just in time."

She turned to him and took his hand. "I'm glad. Driving is very hard. That was smart thinking."

"We found Mrs. Cooper, but we didn't get the Christmas tree."

Stunned, she looked at Virgil. "You found Ester. Where? Is she okay?"

"She was in an abandoned cabin on the other side of Black Water Creek. She was alive so I tried to carry her back to the car to get help. That's when I fell through the bridge deck."

"What happened to Ester?"

"She's in the hospital in critical condition. Her father and daughter are with her."

"I hope she makes it." Cora inwardly shivered. "Was she hurt?"

"No, it seems someone took her there and just abandoned her."

Cora's eyes widened in disbelief. "Alone, in this weather?"

"That's what it looks like."

"It's a miracle you and Jack found her."

"I have to be honest. I haven't been to that area since I was a teenager."

"Why were you there?"

"To get the Christmas tree," Jack said, as if she should've known. "We found the perfect one. You would've loved it, but I don't want to go back there. We'll find another one."

They arrived home and inside the house, they both helped Jack out of his coat. "Are you hungry?" Cora asked. "I have some soup I can heat up. The baked chicken was a little dry."

Jack rubbed his tummy. "Soup sounds good." He looked at Virgil. "You must be hungry too."

Virgil smoothed his hair then carefully removed his coat. "Only if there's some crackers to go with it."

They went into the kitchen and Cora tried to calm her inner anxiety. Virgil was right, her nephew was an extraordinary young man.

With the soup cans open and coffee perking, she took out the milk and poured two glasses. Getting out the tin of crackers, she waited for Virgil to come out of the bathroom from washing his hands.

He remained silent as she spooned out the chicken noodle soup. She offered sandwiches but neither showed much interest. They tackled the soup with gusto. "You two must be hungry."

"We missed supper," Virgil said. "By the way, what did we have?"

His tone was gentler and panic subsided. Cora was glad because she wasn't able, after all that had happened, to deal with any more. "We had baked chicken. Arthur came by looking for you."

Virgil looked up. "It was probably about Ester."

"Earl talked to him about several things including the report on the mine. Arthur didn't seem too happy about it. He mentioned firing his crew chief."

"He should."

Jack yawned and Cora helped him out of his chair. "You've had a very busy night. It's time for bed."

"Yeah, I'm tired."

She got him to bed in record time. He didn't utter one complaint and she was grateful. Sitting on the edge of his bed, she brushed back his hair and thanked God that he had been returned safely to her. Pal jumped on the bed and inched forward until his nose was buried in Jack's neck.

Virgil's voice came from behind her. "He's quite a boy."

"I agree." She looked at Virgil. "I'm sorry if you were angry with me for being overprotective. You and Jack mean everything to me."

"I feel the same way, but we have to let the boy grow up, make mistakes and learn to use his head. This incident was a perfect example."

"How?"

He walked over to her and sat on the edge of the bed. "I kept thinking about him, you and our unborn baby. I feared what it would be like if you had to go on without me. It scared me and at the same time it made me determined to get out of there for you."

She took his hand. "I'm glad Jack helped you."

"I can't tell you how frightened I was that I might not be coming home. But worse, I didn't want Jack to think that he'd failed."

"I understand."

"Cora, he showed more bravery than a grown man and he had the presence of mind to come up with a plan and implement it. That's a sign of greatness."

"I hope that you're not considering he go into the military. I never want Jack to fight to stay alive."

"Neither do I, but I wouldn't rule out him going to a really good college."

"I've always wanted that for him."

"Good, now we both are going in the same direction."

"When I said I didn't want him taking chances, that was the mother in me speaking. I'll always feel that way."

He stood, leaned down and kissed her on the top of the head. "I'm going to bed. I'm exhausted."

"I'll straighten the kitchen and be right in."

He took off his shirt and stuck his hand though the hole in the back. "I don't suppose you can mend this?"

She took it from him and held it out. "Heavens no, it's ruined." She took him by the arm and turned him around. Gently she peeled back the bandage and saw the stitched wound. "You're lucky no internal organs were injured. Did Stan say anything?"

"No, just keep it covered and clean." Virgil rubbed his hip. "He gave me a shot too."

"Good, then you'll be fine." She wiggled her finger at him. "But no walking across broken bridges anymore, you hear? I don't want you taking chances either." She looked at him and grinned. "That's the wife in me speaking."

He smiled and ducked into the bedroom. Before going to bed she called the hospital and talked to Stan. Ester was in critical condition, but he thought she might make it. Another few hours exposed to the cold and she would have fallen victim to the elements.

Cora sat down on the couch with needle and thread to patch the tear in Virgil's jacket. Tears coursed down her cheeks at the thought of losing the two males she cared so much for. With each stitch, her heart tightened and she struggled to breathe.

She simply couldn't go on without them. She clutched the coat to her face and breathed in Virgil's scent, making her heart accelerate. She loved him so much.

CHAPTER TWENTY-EIGHT

Virgil woke to a stiff back and sore muscles. He stretched several times before rolling over to the edge of the bed and putting his feet on the cold floor.

"Are you okay?"

"I've felt better." Virgil put his hand on his back and straightened. "That hurts."

She came to his side and took his arm. "Maybe a day in bed will do you good."

"I have too much to do for that." He pulled on his pants and a clean shirt. As he struggled with the buttons, she slapped his hand away and finished the job. "First burns then blisters and now splinters. Your hands are a mess."

Leaning down he kissed her softly then asked, "Have you checked on Ester today?"

"Yes, and she's about the same."

"Talking yet?"

"No, and there isn't much of a chance she will for a while."

"I want to talk to her as soon as I can. She's the only one who can identify her kidnapper."

Jack hesitated to enter the bedroom. His hair neatly combed, his shirt tucked into jeans with a belt he'd yet to grow into. "You okay?" he asked Virgil. "Can I come in?" Jack's face was pale and solemn.

Virgil motioned with his hand. "Sure, you can."

"I wanted to say we still need to get a Christmas tree."

"You're right and we'll get one this weekend."

"I don't want the one on the other side of the creek."

Virgil shook his head, leaned down and put his hand on Jack shoulder. "No, we're not ever going back there. We'll find another tree."

A look of complete relief covered Jack's face. "Good," he said darting out of the room. "Tommy's here. I'm leaving."

Virgil looked at Cora. Seeing the pain in her eyes and pulled her closer. "He's going to be all right. Have a little faith."

"I'm trying my best, but I could have lost both of you." She pulled from his embrace wiping away tears. "Come into the kitchen. Your breakfast is ready."

The smell of bacon woke up his appetite and had his mouth watering. After an awkward shave at the bathroom sink, he went to the table where Earl sat enjoying a cup of coffee, two eggs, bacon and homemade biscuits. Cora slid the same plate in front of him.

Pouring herself some coffee, she sat down to a piece of toast. Earl shoved half a fried egg into his mouth and chewed slowly. As he picked up a biscuit, which he spread liberally with apple butter, he asked. "How're you feeling today, Virgil? Heard you got a pretty big hole in your back."

"I know it's there."

"Well, thank God you didn't fall in that water."

"I'm grateful, all right."

"You not taking the day off?"

"No, I'm hoping Ester wakes up so I can question her. Until that happens, Ethan and I are going to check out that cabin."

"No," Cora said. "I don't want you back on that bridge."

"I'm taking my waders. I'll cross closer to town where the water's pretty shallow."

"Just don't get hurt."

"I can't always guarantee that, but I'll do my best." He smiled. It wasn't easy being a sheriff and he realized there was always a chance he wouldn't come home at night, but he didn't dwell on that.

"I can't for the life of me remember the name of the man who lived in that cabin. Only saw him a few times." Earl smacked his lips. "He wasn't from around here. I don't even think that property is deeded."

"Part of that area was put aside for mining but was never developed because the ground wasn't that stable."

"I remember when that happened. But years before the loner showed up, a man by the name of Wilcox farmed that land. Don't know if he owned it or not, but he grew wheat out there," Earl said.

"I'll check the county records."

Virgil finished his breakfast and offered Cora a ride to work. Earl said he'd do the dishes. As they walked out the door the sound of a plate crashing to the floor echoed through the house. Cora sighed and rolled her eyes. "I repaired your coat, but you're going to need a new one."

"It sounds like we might need to buy some new dishes, too." He gave her a hot kiss and ducked out the door.

At the office, Ethan waited impatiently. "You ready to go?"

"Yeah, just give me a minute. I'm not moving real fast today."

"I'm surprised you're still alive. Damn, Virgil. I thought you were a goner."

Virgil rubbed his face. "I don't even like to think about it. Jack really proved to be quite the hero."

"He's sharp, that boy."

Virgil grinned at the thought of Jack struggling to save his life. Before they could get out the door, Francis came in and asked to speak to Virgil. After the door was closed, Virgil took the chair behind his desk.

Francis stood. "When you went out to Ida's house the night she shot her husband, what did she say?"

"That he'd been mean to her and her children and she had no way out."

"But she never came to the law?"

Virgil went to lean back, this remembered his back. "No, she told John and according to her, he went out there and talked to Ervin."

"You don't know what John said to him?"

"I wasn't the sheriff at that time." Virgil leaned forward. "But she told me after John talked to her husband he beat her worse than ever. Said she couldn't get up off the floor for two days."

"I wish she'd confided in you."

"That night she told me she threatened to, but Ervin swore he'd shoot me in the back and it would be her fault. That's what kept her quiet."

Francis perked up. "So she brought her problem to the law, and threatened to do it again, but was physically forced to abandon her idea?"

"I don't know that Ervin physically threatened her about shooting me in the back, but she believed he'd do it."

"I may need you to testify in court."

"I will if you need me to."

"I think we have enough to prove Ida was a victim of abuse and brainwashed so badly she wasn't thinking straight. No jury can condemn a woman who fears for herself and her children."

"I don't think you'll have a problem here in Gibbs City. The problem will be if you have to move the trial out of the county."

"I want to avoid a trial altogether if I can."

Virgil didn't know about that. A man died and usually there had to be an accounting for that. "Francis I know you want to protect Ida and her girls. I admire you for that, but don't think Ervin Butcher's murder will be dismissed without due process."

The judge let out a deep troubling breath. "I just hate her going through all that."

"I understand, but if it isn't cleared up now, it could come back later and cause a problem." Virgil stood. He had to search the cabin and go to the hospital to see how Ester was doing. "I suggest you speak to JJ. See what he can do for you. He's a smart man with a lot of pull. You do too much and people will start thinking you're trying to cover up the truth."

Francis stood. "You're right." He ran his hand over the brim of his hat. "What have you found out so far about Hilda's murder and Ester's kidnapping?"

"Not much yet. I'm questioning her husband Mitch and his brother."

"Gilbert?"

"He was one of the last people who saw her alive."

"The brothers are pretty close. I imagine they're both grieving."

"We'll see."

"How'd Arthur take the report?"

"He's not happy from what Earl says. I think he'll do the right thing."

After Francis left, Virgil and Ethan decided to get out of the office before anyone else came in. They were both anxious to get out to Black Water Creek and see if they could find any clues as to who kidnapped Ester.

Pulling up near to the area where they'd found Hilda's body, Virgil and Ethan got out of the car. As they made their way to the bank of the creek, they found Mitch standing exactly where his wife's body had been found.

"What are you doing here?" Virgil asked.

"I learned this is where her body was found." He put his bare hands in the pockets of his jacket. "I thought if I came here I'd feel closer to her." He looked at them, tears brimming over his eyes. "I miss her so much." He averted his gaze. "And to learn we were going to have a baby. It's just too much."

Virgil clasped his shoulder and said, "I think you need to go home and be with your family. There's nothing here."

Mitch looked out over the creek. "I guess you're right. I just wanted to be close to her so I could feel her presence one more time."

Virgil and his deputy watched the broken man walk away. He hadn't driven his car, and home was a long walk, but he probably needed that to clear his head.

Ethan stepped into the water. "It's a shame this all had to happen."

"Yeah, I'll be glad when this is over with." They waded into the deepest part of the creek and Virgil felt the fast moving water push against his legs. He stopped.

"Did the ME say how long Hilda was in the water?"

Ethan stopped and looked back. "I don't think he said she was in the water." Ethan turned to face him. "He would've mentioned that if she had been, wouldn't he?"

"I didn't see any signs of her body being wet except for the snow. You don't think she could've been killed downstream and the current carried the body here, do you?"

"When they took her away, she didn't look like she'd spent any time in the water. Also, her body was completely out of the creek. If the water had moved her, some part of her would still be in the water."

Virgil started walking. "Let's see what the cabin holds."

They arrived at the cabin and it appeared no one had been there since he and Jack had removed Ester. There were no additional footprints and the door stood ajar like he'd left it.

Ethan carried a long pole and used it to lift debris and branches as he walked the perimeter of the cabin. Virgil stayed close, his eyes taking in everything. Outside, the windows hadn't been touched and the place was exactly as he left it. Inside, nothing had changed. He moved a few things with the toes of his waders but uncovered nothing.

He studied the interior with an eye trained to find the unusual, yet everything appeared normal for an abandoned shack. There was nothing of use. The place was small, filthy and littered with broken furniture, rags and trash. There wasn't a hint of who'd last been there.

Ethan came in. "Nothing out there. If there were prints at one time the snow covered them up pretty good."

"What do you think happened here?"

"Well, with the chair overturned, I'd say someone kidnapped her, tied her up and then just left, leaving her here to die, slowly. Like you said, even if she could've gotten away, the door was bolted and no one but a small child could fit through these windows."

"Who would do that?"

"We've been asking that for days."

"In my gut, something tells me that Hilda's murder and Ester's abduction were connected."

"They both happened the same day." Ethan looked outside and shook his head. "Pretty damn close to each other and the two were friends."

"We've got some sick SOB running around loose in Gibbs City."

CHAPTER TWENTY-NINE

Cora entered the hospital and wasted no time finding Ester's room number and making her way in that direction. She entered to find an exhausted Arthur and Alice sitting close enough to hold each other's hand. "How's she doing?"

Always the gentleman, Arthur stood. "She's just started to mumble things. She's not really awake but Dr. Lowery said it was an improvement. No word that she's out of the woods yet."

"I'm sure he'll keep you briefed on her condition." Cora took Ester's pale hand and noticed the ugly rope burns on her wrists. "She's very strong. She'll make it."

"I hope you're right, Miss Cora," Alice said. "I'd hate to lose my mother."

Cora imagined the girl suffered badly because it wasn't that long ago that she'd lost her father. And while Bart Cooper was a despicable man, she felt sure Alice loved him. "Just have faith."

She left and went to her office, hung up her coat and slipped on her lab coat to make her rounds. She'd no sooner reached for the door when Dr. Adams came in, anger twisting in his face. "I saw you in there with Dr. Lowery's patient. You just can't keep your nose out of other people's business can you?"

"Every patient in this hospital is my business and Ester Cooper is a personal friend." She moved forward. "Now get out of my way and don't come back to my office."

He grabbed her wrists. "I'll do what I damn well please and if you don't like it you might end up in basement with the rest of the corpses."

"Let me go," she yelled.

"You bitch."

The door opened and Earl stepped inside. "Morning Cora," he said calmly. "I came by to check on Ester. Thought I'd say hello to you while I was here."

Dr. Adams released her and Cora staggered back against her desk. "I was just leaving."

"No you ain't." Earl shut the door with his cane. "You ain't going nowhere but out the front door. You're fired for assaulting a fellow doctor."

"I didn't assault her."

"You did because I saw you." Earl opened the door. "Follow me, Adams."

Shaken, Cora slumped back on her desk, her heart racing. Adams was definitely not being professional by charging into her office. She clutched her throat. For the first time since Warren Hayes held her captive, Cora feared for her life. His hatred was irrational.

After taking a moment to compose herself, she walked out of her office. She turned then noticed that the storage room door was ajar. She stepped closer and heard a man talking.

Peeking inside, she saw Earl had Dr. Adams by the front of his shirt in a heated argument. Earl pulled Dr. Adams closer and said, "If you so much as touch a hair on her head, I'll cut you in so many pieces they'll never be able to put you back together again."

Stepping closer, Cora was taken back by Earl's brazen act. And if Adam's eyes said anything, he was scared out of his wits. Was Earl serious? It appeared so.

"Now I want you out of this hospital in one hour. Then I want you out of town in twenty four hours. I don't want to ever see your face again," Earl gritted out, shoving Dr. Adams against the wall. "Now git out of here and don't ever come back."

Swallowing hard, Cora hurried away before they saw her and everyone would be embarrassed. Shocked at her neighbor's behavior, she straightened her coat and headed for her rounds. As she stood at the nurse's station Earl approached. "You see that guy again, let me know. I'm notifying the board that he's no longer employed here."

"Believe me when I say, I'm sorry about that, Earl."

"You didn't do anything wrong, Missy. We don't need people like Adams in this hospital."

"There isn't a person in the hospital he doesn't hassle. And to be honest, Nurse Hill isn't any better."

"Don't you worry. I'll take care of her. First I want to visit Arthur. Then I'm making sure Adams gets out of town."

"You don't have to do that. I'm sure he'll leave."

"Just to make sure." He grinned. "Don't fret."

She looked at Ester's room. "I think she's beginning to come around."

"Good. Poor Arthur needs some good news."

"Thank God Virgil found her."

"I'm glad he and Jack made it out of there alive."

She placed her hand to her heart. "Don't remind me. It still makes my knees weak and my heart flutter."

"It scared the living hell out of me."

"Virgil should be here any minute. He'll want to talk to Ester to see what she remembers."

"I hope he can get to the bottom of all this and life can get back to normal around here."

She chuckled. "Normal? What's that?"

Earl went into the patient's room and Stan came up to her. "I hear Dr. Adams has been fired."

"News sure travels fast."

"He immediately ran to Dr. Janson," Stan said, shoving his hands in his pockets. "Expect a fight."

Cora held up her hands. "I didn't do anything. Earl Clevenger is the one who sent him packing."

"He's blaming it all on you."

"Of course, he is."

"Don't worry. I told Janson I would stand by you on this matter and we should let the board decide."

"I just want him to leave me alone."

"A man like Adams doesn't know how to do that. He's a bully and a pusher, so it's best if he moves on."

It wasn't long after Earl went into Ester's room that she saw Nurse Price who told her Virgil had just come in searching for Ester.

Worried about him, she went to Ester's room and found Virgil standing next to the bed. Moving quietly she walked up next to him and touched his hand. "How are you doing?"

"I'm fine," he said, trying to smile. "Has she said anything?"

"No," Arthur said. "Alice and I have been trying to wake her up, but the doctor says she's not ready yet."

"I'm anxious to talk to her. Only she can identify the guilty party."

"I hope she can remember," Arthur said. "And if Ollie Ruth doesn't leave me and my family alone I'm pressing charges. The man's a nuisance. He came up here today but the nurses wouldn't let him in."

"What's he doing here?"

Arthur shook his head. "I have no idea, but I want him away from my family." He held out his hands to Virgil. "What if he decides to come in here tonight and do something to Ester just to spite me?"

"I'll take care of that," Virgil said. Cora saw the lines bracketing his mouth tighten. "He won't be up here again."

Cora placed the back of her hand on Ester's forehead. She was cool to the touch. "I'm sure it won't be long. She's been through a horrible ordeal. But her vitals are improving."

Virgil turned to her. "As soon as she wakes up, call me." He turned and left.

She smiled up at Arthur. "Be thankful she was found in time."

Arthur walked over and wrapped his arms around her. "I'm so grateful to Virgil for being the best sheriff this town could ever ask for." He stepped back taking her hand. "I hear little Jack was quite the hero."

"Yes," she replied weakly. "And I don't want him to ever do that again." She pressed her hand against her chest. "Ever."

"I don't blame you." Arthur looked at Ester's still body. "We tend to love our children more than anything in the world."

"And we don't want them in danger."

Alice came closer. "Do you think my mom will be okay?"

"There's a good possibility that she'll be fine and be able to leave the hospital soon. There was no head trauma or physical abuse. We're fighting the effects the cold weather had on her while she was held in the cabin."

Alice broke down and Arthur took her in his arms. "She'll be okay, dear."

"What if she had died? I hate living in a place where things like this happen."

"I know, but Virgil will find the person responsible and bring him to justice. We can't stop bad things from happening, that's not how life works."

Cora left the room and finished her rounds. Ester was safe and the family would be reunited. She couldn't help but wonder if Ollie Ruth was the guilty party in all this. It appeared he wanted Arthur to suffer and nothing could be more demoralizing than losing your only child. But in a way, that's exactly what happened to the Ruth family.

As she entered the hall she ran into JJ. "Hello, how are you?"

"I'm fine," he replied. He didn't look like he had good news. "Can we go to your office?"

Once there she closed the door and looked at her cousin. "What's the matter?"

He was dressed in his usual suit and freshly starched shirt. He looked his part as the Assistant District Attorney. "I received a call from Ann Martin's lawyer demanding you turn over Jack or face a trial."

She straightened her spine. "I'll see them all dead before I give up my nephew to them."

"I told him as much, but that didn't deter him. Says his client has a right to the boy and she's willing to go as far as necessary to get him."

"Good. Let her." Cora's heart thudded loudly and her head spun. "He's mine and I won't ever let him go."

"You may not have a choice. I'm working to make sure if we go to trial it's held here in Parker County. We'd stand a better chance. Everyone here knows what a good person you are and how much you love Jack."

"But a father is his closest relative."

JJ propped his foot on a nearby chair, and leaned forward. "That's true, but as far as I can see, Dan Martin doesn't even have a job and hasn't filed taxes in ten years."

Cora folded her arms. "What does that mean?"

JJ grinned, showing a mouthful of perfect white teeth. "Tax evasion."

She shrugged. "So, he didn't pay taxes. That doesn't mean anything."

His grin changed to a broad smile. "It did to Al Capone."

CHAPTER THIRTY

Virgil drove to Ollie Ruth's house on 7th Street. It really wasn't much of a place. Hardly more than a tarpapered hovel that looked like a good gust of wind would blow it down. The Ruths were dirt poor and the old man had done little to alleviate that. He'd worked in the mines off and on for a few years but not much else.

They basically lived off what their oldest son, Sam, had made. By now, their son would have been old enough to have his own family, but Virgil was sure his parents discouraged that because they needed his money. Now that he was gone, Ollie and his wife were no doubt hoping to sue Arthur.

The engineers' report put the lid on that. While they could most likely expect some compensation from the owner of the mine, they wouldn't be able to financially ruin Arthur. And people like Ollie Ruth lived for those kinds of opportunities.

Virgil knocked on the door and waited. Ollie finally opened the door, his thinning hair uncombed, barely dressed in long johns and pants that were held up by suspenders. His feet were dirty and bare.

"What do you want, Sheriff?"

"I want to ask you a few questions."

Ollie didn't have the decency to invite him in. "What about?"

"Ester Cooper."

"I thought she was dead."

"No, she was missing. But we found her."

His eyes narrowed. "That's too bad. I was hoping someone had dumped her down an abandoned mine shaft."

"Maybe that's where we found her."

"I don't care where you found her, or where she was. Now get off my property unless you're here to arrest me."

"Why would I arrest you, Ollie?"

"Why wouldn't you? Ain't you a friend of old Arthur Bridges? I heard you're good buddies."

Virgil nodded. "Yes, he's a friend, and while I'm not here to arrest anyone, I am here to say that if you step foot on his property again, you'll be arrested and charged for trespassing until Judge Garner can decide what to do."

"That's another good friend of yours."

"I have a lot of friends, Ollie. While I don't count you among them, that doesn't mean you haven't been treated fairly. I won't allow you to go around terrorizing and threatening the people of my community."

"I was just letting off a little steam. My boy died. I got the right to grieve."

"No, you're disturbing the peace and I won't tolerate that kind of nonsense. I respect that you've lost your son and that's a terrible thing, but that doesn't give you the right to harass Arthur Bridges."

"All I can say is he better damn well be generous or I'll raise all kinds of trouble."

"You already have. After all, someone kidnapped Ester. Who better than the man who lost his son in a mine? Good way to punish the owner."

Ollie staggered back. "You think I took her?" He pointed his finger at Virgil. "Don't you go blaming me for something I didn't do, you hear?"

"I'll do whatever I please until the guilty man is brought to justice. That's what I do, Ollie." Virgil turned and stepped off the porch. "Don't go around Arthur or his family unless you want to go to jail."

The door behind him slammed and Virgil got into this squad car. He didn't know for sure if Ollie Ruth had anything to do with Ester's kidnapping but it sure stood to reason that he had motive. Nothing would make Ruth happier than to see Arthur suffer.

He arrived at the office to find Ida Butcher waiting for him. She looked very nice in a new dress, shoes, her hair shinny and clean. Her hands had lost some of the roughness and it appeared she'd gained a pound or two. "What can I do for you, Mrs. Butcher?"

"I'd like to speak privately, if we can?"

Virgil and Ethan shared a questioning glance then he opened the door to his office and invited her in. She took a seat while he went around to the other side of his desk and sat. "You need something?"

"I want you to be honest with me because Francis hasn't been."

Virgil leaned back and propped his elbows on the arms of his chair. "Oh?"

"I know why he's being so kind and I want to make sure his thoughtfulness isn't getting him in trouble."

"There's very little that can get a judge in trouble, Mrs. Butcher. Plus, he knows the law inside and out."

"But would he break it to save me?"

"I honestly don't think he would. He might try everything in his power to keep you from going to prison, but he would never cross that line."

She let out a troubling breath. "I'm glad to hear that," she said. "I was so worried I'd be the reason he'd get disbarred or something dreadful."

"He's a good man."

"He's too good."

"Mrs. Butcher..."

"Call me Ida. I don't like the name Butcher."

"Okay, Ida. I think it's best if you just let Francis do what he has to do. He's meeting with JJ and together they'll come up with as good a case as they can to prove Ervin was killed in self-defense."

"Do juries really believe that?"

Virgil laced his fingers. "I don't always know what a jury is thinking. I've seen a lot of surprises in court, but I'm prepared to state that your life and that of your two daughters were in danger. That Ervin was a cruel, callous man who told you he'd shoot me in the back if you reported him."

"Will that be enough?"

"I have no idea. But, you shouldn't worry. Let Francis take care of you until this is over. Then go live your life, Ida. You deserve that much."

She looked down at her folded hands. "He's asked me to stay with him." Lifting her eyes, their gazes met. "I think he wants to marry me."

"That's not my business and I prefer not to get involved. But, in my personal opinion, you're both entitled to a little happiness."

Ida stood, shook his hand and turned to go. "Thank you, Sheriff Carter. You've eased my mind a great deal."

"Stop by anytime, Ida. You're always welcome here."

She left his office, nodded to Ethan and closed the door. Ethan looked at him, his eyes wide.

"What's going on," Virgil asked. "You hear something?"

"Miss Cora just called. "Ester is awake and able to talk."

"Let's go."

CHAPTER THIRTY-ONE

Cora stood next to Ester's bed, taking her pulse when Virgil and Ethan charged through the door. Cora held up her hand. "She's very weak. You can't expect too much from her this soon."

"I just have a few questions," Virgil replied. "But they're important."

Cora nodded, and Arthur stepped back.

Virgil approached slowly, Ethan right behind him. "Ester, I'm glad you're okay."

She held out her limp hand. "Thank you," she said hoarsely. "Daddy said you saved me."

Virgil looked at Cora then Ethan. "I just found you. The staff at the hospital saved you."

He took her hand and Cora's pride in her husband grew. He was a man who took his job seriously and really worked hard for the people of this community. Even going so far as to put his own life in jeopardy.

"Can you tell me who took you to that cabin?"

She licked her dry lips. "No, I didn't see anything."

Virgil glanced at Ethan who shook his head. "Nothing?"

"I was out there to meet Hilda. When she didn't show I got out of my car and called out to her."

"Why were you and Hilda meeting out there so far from everything?"

Cora noticed that Ester grew uncomfortable under Virgil's interrogation. "I...I can't say."

Cora stepped forward. "She just woke up. You can't push her too far."

Virgil stared down at the middle aged woman in the hospital bed. "Do you know that Hilda was murdered?"

"What," Ester screamed. "No, that's a lie."

Virgil shook his head. "It's the truth. Someone hit her in the head hard enough to kill her."

Tears filled Ester's eyes. She covered her face. "I can't believe it."

"It's best you go now, Virgil," Cora said. "Give her a few hours. Maybe she'll feel better then."

He looked at her, his expression filled with frustration. "There's a killer out there and she's the only witness I have."

"She didn't see anything," Cora stated. "She can't tell you want she didn't see."

"No doubt she saw more than she thinks or knows something that can help."

Arthur stepped closer to them. "I want to get to the bottom of this. A woman is dead and one was kidnapped. Ester needs to tell Virgil everything she knows."

Cora nodded and walked over and took Ester's arms and removed her hands from her face. "Please answer the Sheriff's questions. The person who did this should be found before someone else is hurt."

Ester gripped the edge of the white sheet covering her body. "Hilda wanted to return to Germany."

"Mitch told me that," Virgil said, impatiently.

She lowered her eyes. "She was expecting."

"We know that as well."

Ester looked away. "I was meeting Hilda to take her to get rid of the baby."

Cora leaned down. Thinking of her own child, she found the thought of someone willingly getting an abortion difficult to understand. "Why would she do that?"

"She'd hidden back enough money to go to Germany. Her papers had arrived from the US Department of Immigration. But she didn't want to go back to her family carrying a child. She was afraid her family would throw her out."

Ethan cocked his head and folded his arms. "How'd she get permission to leave?"

"She had her mother write a letter saying her family needed her. They'd lied and said she would only be gone thirty days."

"But she had no intentions of coming back to Mitch?" Virgil asked. "She was going to stay there."

Ester twisted the sheets, using the corner to dab away her tears. "No, she'd never loved him. He was just a way out of the country to her."

"Do you think Mitch could've murdered his wife?"

"He didn't know anything." Ester sat up. "She'd been really careful to keep the whole thing a secret. I was the only person she confided in."

Ester grabbed Virgil's hand. "Please don't tell Mitch she was going to get rid of his child. I tried to talk her out of it, but she wouldn't listen."

Virgil patted her hand. "I can't promise anything at this point."

Arthur stepped closer. "But, what happened to you?"

Ester shook her head. "I don't know. Someone came up behind me, put a cloth to my mouth and the next thing I knew, I woke up and I was tied to a chair in a cabin I'd never been in before."

"I found you on the floor," Virgil said.

"I deliberately tipped over the chair when I saw the clothing around the floor. I was freezing and figured if I didn't get some kind of cover, I'd die from exposure."

Cora took her hand from Virgil's and laid it on the bed. "You did the right thing. That one move probably saved your life."

"And you don't remember anything else. No one ever came back to check on you?"

"No, and I screamed my head off until I lost my voice." She looked at her father. "Where was I?"

"Out by the bend in Black Water Creek. Near the old bridge."

"So, I wasn't far from my car?"

"No, but the problem is, who knew you were there?"

"I didn't tell anyone."

Cora put her hand on Virgil's back. "Let's let her rest. She's exhausted. Maybe she'll remember more tomorrow."

Virgil and Ethan nodded as they headed out the door. Cora pulled the blanket up Ester's chest. "You get some rest." She looked at Arthur and Alice. "Take Alice home. I don't want either of you to end up in the bed beside her."

"I think we might if you're sure she'll be okay."

"I'm sure she will be fine. With rest and good food, she'll be home in no time."

Arthur and Alice kissed Ester goodbye and left. "I feel so bad for Hilda. She was so lonely and wanted to go home so much."

"I can't say what would've been the best way to have handled all this, and I know Hilda was your friend, but she should've been honest with her husband."

"How easy would it be for you to tell Virgil you didn't love him?"

Cora thought for a long time. She couldn't imagine not loving Virgil with all her heart. Could she inflict that kind of pain on him? The one thing she knew was that she'd never abort his child.

"I'm not sure your abduction and Hilda's murder are connected. If they are, Virgil hasn't found that out yet. Are you sure you didn't see or hear anything?"

"No, it was snowing really hard. I was tempted to go to Hilda's house. I didn't because I was afraid I'd miss her along the way. So I waited."

"I remember you were depressed when you left that afternoon. Did you talk to anyone?"

"No, Reverend Washburn offered help with the Women's Prayer Meeting, but I told him that wasn't necessary."

"So, no one knew where you were going when you left my house that afternoon?"

Ester shook her head. "I just stepped out of my car. For a minute I thought I saw Hilda coming toward me, but I wasn't sure."

"Get some rest and you'll feel better tomorrow. I'll order something to help you sleep."

Ester brushed away tears. "Thank you, Cora. Thank you for being such a good friend."

"You just think about getting better."

Her shift ended and soon Cora left for home. She smiled as she passed the homes decorated for Christmas. There were homemade nativity scenes, cedar trees covered with tinsel, wooden candy canes in the yards and lit candles in the windows with wreaths hanging on doors.

She arrived home to look at the house. It looked drab and forlorn compared to the other homes. Her family would spend this weekend decorating outside so their place would look as festive and scenic as the others she'd passed. Going to Maggie's to get Jack she waved at Susan Welch and Ronnie as they made their way home from the market. Ronnie had grown so much lately.

At Maggie's she opened the door to the rich aroma of homemade yeast rolls in the oven. "That smells delicious."

"Good, I made an extra batch." She handed Cora a basket full of fresh rolls. "I wasn't sure what you had planned for supper, but everyone in my house loves those with whatever I cook."

"The same for us. Thank you so much."

As Jack put on his coat, Maggie asked, "How's Ester?"

"She's going to be fine. Just tired and we're keeping an eye on her for signs of exposure."

"Who did it?"

Cora shrugged. "She didn't see anyone. I guess the person walked up behind her and put a cloth over her mouth. It was probably doused in chloroform."

"That's strange. How many people have access to that besides doctors?"

"I don't know. I'm just guessing. That would be the most likely to make a person unconscious."

"I hope Virgil finds out who did it. It's frightening to know there's a killer out there."

Cora gripped her coat tighter around her. "It sure is." She held up the basket. "Thank you so much. I owe you a pie this weekend."

"Don't worry about it."

Cora walked in the house to find Virgil and Earl setting the table. She'd put on a pot of beans in her pressure cooker knowing they'd be done by the time she got home from work.

She noticed Virgil had removed his uniform and only wore his undershirt and a pair of pants. She'd check the wound on his back after dinner.

"Look," she said, holding up the basket. "Maggie made fresh rolls."

She put them on the table, peeled potatoes to fry while Earl and Virgil helped Jack out of his coat and school clothes then she put on fresh coffee.

"Did you talk to Ollie Ruth today?" Earl asked. "If you didn't, I will."

"I went to his house and had a talk with him."

"I think he's behind all this."

"He's certainly got the temperament."

Virgil looked at her. "How was Ester when you left?"

"She's exhausted. I sent Arthur and Alice home and ordered a sleeping sedative for her tonight."

"I wonder why Ester and Hilda decided to meet in such an isolated place."

"Ester said she thought she saw Hilda coming toward her, but wasn't sure because of the snow. Someone put a cloth probably soaked with chloroform to render her unconscious."

Virgil took a sip of coffee. "So, Hilda might have witnessed Ester's abduction."

Earl looked at Virgil and raised a brow. "And if she turned to run away."

Looking at Earl, Virgil said, "The killer hit her from behind."

After the meal, Jack took his bath and went to bed, Virgil, Earl and Cora sat at the kitchen table talking. Earl asked, "Do you think there is a connection between Hilda being killed and Ester getting kidnapped?"

"If there is, I can't find it. They weren't too far apart, but why kill one and kidnap the other?"

"I think the person who did this left Ester there as a statement. Could be they didn't mean to kill Hilda."

"That's for sure and the main reason I think Ollie Ruth is to blame, but in all honesty he doesn't act like a man who killed one woman and kidnapped another."

"Well, he hates Arthur," Cora said.

"And he wants him to suffer," Earl added. "And he's mean."

"But does Ollie Ruth have access to medical supplies?"

CHAPTER THIRTY-TWO

"I have Ethan watching Ruth's house tonight," Virgil said. "I wasn't counting on Ester being at the hospital alone."

"Do you think she's in danger?" Cora asked.

Virgil stood, shoved back his chair and slipped on his shirt and coat. He removed his gun and holster from the top of the fridge.

"I've got a hunch. I'll feel better checking on her. Don't wait up, sweetheart. Get some rest. Earl will keep an eye on the place. Without saying anything else, he walked out, got into his squad car and headed for the hospital.

He drove as fast as he could. It was already dark and visiting hours were over. He arrived, parked in the back parking lot and ran inside. He arrived at Ester's room to find the night nurse standing beside the bed.

"Evening sheriff. Visiting hours are over."

"I plan to stick around for a while."

The nurse, a young girl fresh out of nursing school who'd moved to Gibbs City for a job, nodded. "I just gave her something to help her sleep, so she probably can't answer any questions."

"I don't want to talk to her."

Confused, the nurse smiled and left the room, closing the door behind her. Virgil took the ladder-back chair and put it behind the door and waited.

In the darkness he continued to listen as the hospital grew quiet. Visitors left, nurses made their final rounds, and the lights were lowered. Only necessary staff worked at night. Doctors were home and called in when there were emergencies.

He straightened when he heard the soft shuffling of hard-soled shoes. He stood and put his hand on the handle of his gun. As the door silently slid open he pressed his back against the wall and gritted his teeth. He stepped out just as the shape of a man lifted the extra pillow on the bed beside Ester over his head.

Flipping on the light, Virgil said, "Hold it right there, Lyle."

Surprised, Lyle Watters turned to him and pulled a gun from his pocket. "You're like a damn dog on a bone. You couldn't leave it alone."

"Put the gun down and come with me. You're under arrest for the murder of Hilda Weaver and kidnapping Ester Cooper."

"I had to do it." He licked his lips. "I wanted the great Arthur Bridges to know what it felt like to lose a child you love and to know she suffered."

"Nobody had to die, Lyle. Arthur didn't cause that mine to cave in. Hilda never hurt anyone and Ester's a good woman."

"Oh yeah, they're all such good people. Getting rich off the dead bodies of our sons. I want those damn mines shut down."

"You don't have the power to do that."

Lyle looked at the sleeping Ester. "She's had everything she's ever wanted."

"She watched cancer eat away at her mother for five years."

"Ha," Lyle thumped himself on the chest. "I buried my son."

"And you killed one innocent woman and nearly killed another."

"I didn't set out to do Hilda Weaver any harm. But she saw me. I had to chase her down and kill her."

"What did you hit her with?"

He held out his gun. "The handle of this."

"Then what did you do?"

"I carried her body downstream for nearly a mile in the freezing water so no one would see the footprints. I didn't know it was going to snow so much."

"Is that why you can barely walk? Your feet are frostbitten."

He hung his head. "Yes. But I couldn't go to no doctor. I was afraid they'd ask too many questions."

Virgil waved his gun toward the door. "Okay, let's go."

Lyle raised the weapon and pointed it at Virgil. "I'll kill you, too. I'm already going to die in prison." He started crying. "Why not kill you and her both?"

"I don't have a good answer for that, but would it make you feel better? Or bring back your son?"

He ran his sleeved arm under his nose then pointed his gun. "It'd make me feel just fine."

Ethan shoved the door open and Virgil took that distraction to pull the trigger. He shot Lyle Watters in the chest. He flew backwards onto the clean bed then slid to the floor. Ester woke screaming and every nurse in the hospital came into the room. But the man was already dead.

"That's mighty good timing Ethan."

"I ran into Leonard Casey, the barber, earlier and he said he saw Lyle hanging around your house Sunday afternoon then when Ester drove away, he followed."

"Leonard didn't think that was important a few days ago."

"He said he never gave it a second thought until late this evening when he saw Lyle leaving his house in a hurry. He called the office and I figured Lyle was either going to Arthur's or the hospital."

"You chose right."

"Oh, I stopped by your house. That's when Cora told me you'd gone to the hospital to check on Ester."

"I'm glad you came in when you did."

"So am I."

"How'd you figure out it was Lyle?"

"Cora told me Ester said the person put a cloth over her mouth until she passed out. Lyle used to work as a janitor here. He knew how to get medical supplies."

CHAPTER THIRTY-THREE

At breakfast the next morning, Cora said, "I want you two to go on Saturday and cut down a Christmas tree. Earl and I are going to be getting the Christmas decorations down from his attic. We're going to have the best Christmas ever."

"That sounds like a good plan," Jack said. "Can I string the popcorn?"

Cora smiled. "You and Virgil are going to do all the decorating."

"Really?" Virgil asked. "You don't plan to help?"

"No, I'm making hot chocolate after I get back from buying your Christmas presents."

"What do you want?" Jack asked.

Cora placed her hand on her stomach and smiled. "I don't know, Jack. How about a little cousin for you?"

"What?"

"Aunt Cora is going to have a baby."

Jack's eyes grew wide. "You are?"

"Yes. How do you feel about that?"

Jack shrugged. "I don't rightly know." His brows wrinkled. "Maybe if you make sure it's a boy 'cause I don't want no girl."

Cora and Virgil shared a startled glance. "We can't promise that. When it comes to babies you don't get a choice," Cora said.

"Well, then we'll just be stuck with whatever we get."

"What do you want for a Christmas present, Jack?"

He thought for a while and Cora felt certain he'd want the big shiny toy fire truck in the dime store window.

"For Christmas I'd like to call Uncle Virgil dad, and you mom." He ducked his head and scrunched his shoulders. "I even wrote Santa."

Cora's heart melted like butter on a stove. "Really?"

Jack looked excited. "Sure, Tommy has a mom and dad and I want one too."

"I think that's fine since your mom and I are going to adopt you as our own."

"Then we'd be a real family."

Cora pulled Jack into her arms. "We've been a family from the very beginning and we always will be."

BOOKS BY GERI FOSTER

THE FALCON SECURITIES SERIES
OUT OF THE DARK
WWW.AMAZON.COM/DP/B00CB8GY9K

OUT OF THE SHADOWS
WWW.AMAZON.COM/DP/B00CB4QY8U

OUT OF THE NIGHT
WWW.AMAZON.COM/DP/BOOF1F7Q9M

OUT OF THE PAST
WWW.AMAZON.COM/DP/BOOJSVTRVU

ACCIDENTAL PLEASURES SERIES

WRONG ROOM
WWW.AMAZON.COM/DP/B00GM9PU94

WRONG BRIDE
WWW.AMAZON.COM/DP/B00N0ZMNSU

WRONG PLAN
WWW.AMAZON.COM/DP/B00MO2RFR8

LOVE RELEASED

WRONG HOLLY
WWW.AMAZON.COM/DP/B00OBS03M2
WRONG GUY
WWW.AMAZON.COM/DP/B00KK94F6G

GERI FOSTER

ABOUT THE AUTHOR

As long as she can remember, Geri Foster has been a lover of reading and the written words. In the seventh grade she wore out two library cards and had read every book in her age area of the library. After raising a family and saying good-bye to the corporate world, she tried her hand at writing.

Action, intrigue, danger and sultry romance drew her like a magnet. That's why she has no choice but to write action-romance suspense. While she reads every genre under the sun, she's always been drawn to guns, bombs and fighting men. Secrecy and suspense move her to write edgy stories about daring and honorable heroes who manage against all odds to end up with their one true love.

You can contact Geri Foster at geri.foster@att.net

Made in the USA
Middletown, DE
07 February 2023

24220342R00119